In His Majesty's Civil Service

In His Majesty's Civil Service

and Other Contemporary Tales of the Kingdom of Bhutan

by

Thomas Slocum

RIVERCROSS PUBLISHING, INC.
New York • Orlando

Printed in the United States of America. No part of this book may be used or reproduced in any manner whatsoever without written permission, except in the case of brief quotations embodied in critical articles and reviews. For information address RIVERCROSS PUBLISHING, INC., 127 East 59th Street, New York, NY 10022 or editor@rivercross.com.

ISBN: 0-944957-98-6

Library of Congress Catalog Card Number: 98-13284

First Printing

Library of Congress Cataloging-in-Publication Data

Slocum, Thomas, 1960-
    In His Majesty's civil service : and other contemporary tales of the kingdom of Bhutan / by Thomas Slocum.
        p.   cm.
    ISBN 0-944957-98-6
    1. Bhutan—Social life and customs—Fiction.   I. Title.
PS3569.L634I5   1998
813'.54—dc21   98-13284
                                                        CIP

Contents

Dasho

The surveyor-in-charge (Building Permit Unit) knocked perfunctorily at the deputy director's office doorway, pulled the curtain aside, and let himself in. "Good morning DD."

The DD slowly lowered the two-week old copy of *The Times of India* that he was reading. "Ah, Mr. Chetri. . . ." He swept his hand towards the cheap, mismatched vinyl chairs in front of his desk. "Please."

Mr. Chetri freed one of the chairs from a bunched-up fold in the faded jute carpet and sat down.

DD folded up his newspaper. "Very cold this morning, isn't it."

"Yes, *la*, very cold."

The DD had been filling the job of acting city manager for a week, but he still occupied his usual cramped office. He wore long underwear under his knee-length *gho* robe against the unseasonably foggy and cold March weather.

Chetri glanced under the desk. "You are having no heater today?"

"It's being fixed."

"Ah."

"Tea?"

"Oh, no sir. Actually, I am going out, la. I am looking for the Hilux driver. Do you know where he is?

"*Achaa*. Dasho took Dilup and the Hilux to Punakha to pick up the *lama* who will perform the spring *puja* at his village this weekend."

Mr. Chetri gazed out the dirt-streaked window across a courtyard where a crew of city street sweepers huddled in shawls and scarves around a small fire. The recently whitewashed wall of the courtyard was already blackened with soot and splattered with blood-red gobs of betel nut spit. "So no vehicle and no driver, isn't it?"

"*Thik chha*."

"Will he be coming back today?"

"No. Not until Monday. What did you need it for?"

Chetri sighed. The city's official policy prohibited personal use of the office Hilux, but it went without saying that the policy did not apply to Dasho. To complain, even to his friend the deputy director, would only invite trouble. "Um, Dasho told me to be taking the survey crew for demarcating the boundary of the new hotel construction site above the river."

"Is there a problem with it?"

"He is thinking that it is encroaching two, three meters onto government land.

"That is *Ashi* Tsetin , the sister of the finance minister's, site, isn't it?"

"Yes la."

"Let's just let that one drop for now. At least until Dasho ah . . . returns to work."

Mr. Chetri waggled his head from side to side and stood up to leave, but DD stopped him. "Stay and have some tea," he said.

"Oh no, la, that's all right."

10

"Yes, yes." He rang the buzzer on his desk. A moment later the office peon peeked his head around the door curtain. *"Duitaa chiyaa,"* ordered the DD. The young man waggled his head and withdrew it back out.

Some time later, as they were sipping their sweet, milky tea, the electrician came in with the repaired heater. It sparked once as he plugged it in, but soon the faint ozone smell vanished and the bar glowed bright orange. Mr. Chetri refolded the front section of DD's paper and set down his china cup and saucer. As he was standing up to leave, he said, "Excuse me, DD, but are you hearing anything about whether Dasho, will be, ah, coming back to work?"

DD set down the sports section and leaned back in his chair. "The Royal Civil Service Commission hasn't made its decision yet. That's all I know."

By three o'clock that afternoon the lama's caravan was working its way in second gear up the last few kilometers of the unpaved road to Jibesa village. At the head of the procession the four wheel drive Toyota Hilux pickup truck from the city manager's office carried the elderly lama, his Pekinese dog, and Dasho. It annoyed Dilip, the driver, that his wash and wax job was now mud-spattered. Behind them fifteen or more red-robed monks, who would assist in the puja, filled two older and even muddier pickups. Older, ordained *gelongs* sat up front in the cabs while the young novices hunched in the trucks' beds. A Maruti Gypsy jeep and three second- or third-hand Toyota Corollas took up the rear. They too were full of people: Jibesa families who now lived in the capital city and had done well enough to buy cars, and who, like Dasho, were returning to the village for the annual spring puja.

At a few places the caravan squeezed around scary gashes that had washed out of the road bed and sloughed mud and rocks down the mountain slope. The drivers had to take one particular corner fast in order not to bog down

11

on the muddy steep section beyond. The second to last Toyota lost traction part way up; gunning the engine and spinning the wheels only settled it deeper into the muddy shoulder. Everyone except grandmother got out of the car to take a look and give the driver advice. Men and boys walked up from the car below and down from the one above and joined in. The car's owner told them to stuff gravel and sticks and brush under the car's back wheels. These shot out behind in a muddy splurt as soon as he gunned it, and everyone got to laughing as they wiped mud off their faces and clothes. Then they all heaved ho against the back bumper and slowly pushed it upwards to where the spinning tires caught good traction.

Dasho sat in the back seat of the Hilux and told the lama how the Jibesa villagers had constructed the road by themselves. In the late eighties some of the village families had pooled their money, bought an old bulldozer and truck, and started a successful contracting company. Then, four years ago, they decided to build this feeder road from the highway. At the time, Dasho had been working as the director of the government's Public Works Department and managed to assign a PWD payloader and dump truck for five months to help with the project. The feeder road to Jibesa had not been included in the Seventh National Five Year Development Plan and the Planning Ministry did not consider it to be a priority. But when his fellow villagers took the initiative themselves, Dasho had been pleased and proud to have done what he could to help them.

The muddy parade rounded the last bend in the road and drove under an arch, draped with yellow cloth, which the villagers had erected to welcome it. By now it was drizzling, but not enough to extinguish the smoking piles of green juniper boughs burning at the sides of the road head. Sweet juniper smoke cleansed the air of evil and unlucky spirits, purifying the village and the people for tomorrow's auspicious puja rituals. Jibesa's four local

12

monks stood at the doorway of the village's small, white-washed temple and blew welcoming blasts on the temple's long horns. Children and adults alike hushed and bowed their heads as Dasho helped the lama from the Hilux.

Jibesa's spring puja would be especially auspicious this year. The venerable, white-haired gentleman whom Dasho had escorted to the village was a *tulku*, the present incarnation of a long line of holy and learned lamas who had successively presided as abbot of one of Bhutan's wealthiest and most prestigious monasteries. This incarnation, Lam Rinchen, had even once served as Bhutan's *Je Khenpo*, the head of the country's state monastic body. It was a blessing for the Jibesa villagers to have this holy man among them. Over the years, Dasho had repeatedly invited him to do a puja here. This spring his persistence had finally paid off; it really was a coup for the village when Lam Rinchen agreed to officiate.

Lam Rinchen blessed each bowed head with a tap of his silk-tasseled wand. A touch of the wand imported great merit to each humble believer, and age-wrinkled and fresh, snotty-nosed faces alike beamed with awe and reverence. During the blessings, Dasho stood by the Hilux straightening his striped wool gho and buckling on his ceremonial sword, an adornment to which his rank entitled him. He gazed across the crowd of villagers, stroking his mustache, and eventually noticed Jibesa's wealthiest farmer in the crowd. He beckoned him over. The farmer bowed and, without waiting for Dasho to ask, assured him that lodging and meals had been prepared for Lam Rinchen and his entourage at his own house. Dasho nodded and clasped his hand warmly. Satisfied that all the arrangements were ready, Dasho bowed to the lama and in short order had him escorted down the path to his lodging. With the lama gone, several villagers now turned to Dasho, bowed, and greeted *"Kuzuzampo la* Dasho." He acknowledged all—relatives, old neighbors and strangers alike—with a slight nod and a smile. As he walked up the familiar path towards his brother's farm house, his sword jouncing on his hip, several followed him, calling more greetings and chattering excitedly about the puja, until they broke off on the paths to their own homes.

Dasho's younger brother Jigme met him half way up the path.

"Kuzuzampo la brother Tshering," he shouted and waved from above.

"Kuzamo brother Jigme," shouted back Dasho. He stopped and caught his breath as Jigme ran down the trail to meet him.

"Sorry brother . . . I didn't greet you down below . . . at the road," Jigme gasped. "I was way up in the back pasture when I heard the monks' horns."

Dasho warmly patted him on the back and laughed softly, "Catch your breath, Jigme, it's no problem." He stood for a moment gazing around at the familiar, unplowed fields and up towards his brother's house. "It's nice to be back here. I wish I came more often."

"We wish you did too brother," said Jigme.

They started up the rest of the path together, but when Dasho fell behind he waved Jigme to go on ahead. It struck him that despite his pounding heart and tired legs, it was the first time in several weeks that he really felt upbeat and confident and serene. He decided that while he was here in Jibesa he would not even think about the unending stream of hassles at the city manager's office, nor about his problem with the civil service commission. No worries at all this weekend. He paused to suck in great breaths of chilly, invigorating mountain air. In the terraced potato field above the house he saw that Jigme's family had set up a cluster of new prayer flags for the spring puja. From the freshly-peeled cedar poles snapped red, blue, and yellow cotton banners of printed scripture, each whipping prayers for prosperity and well-being out over the village.

14

The cluster had been arranged by a local monk, who had consulted Jigme's horoscope to determined the most auspicious colors and arrangement for his flags. Further down the slopes clusters of other colors fluttered outside the neighbors' houses. From way up on the hillside, they reminded Dasho of bouquets of bright flowers.

Dasho trudged up the path through Jigme's kitchen garden to the second story entrance. Like the other farm houses in Jibesa, the bottom story was excavated into the steep hillside and served as a barn for the family's cows and pigs. The house's sturdy, hard-packed mud walls rose to the second story, where the family lived. Next to the door, a notched tree trunk ladder climbed up to the third story, where hay and other provisions were stored. The roof's long, hand-split pine shingles were tied to the purlins by pliant bamboo strips and anchored against the mountain wind by heavy rocks. Wide eaves protected the hayloft from rain and made a shelter for doves, which flew through the open ends and cooed incessantly at dusk and dawn. Only the family's quarters had windows, glassless ones whose thick wood casements and shutters contrasted starkly with the whitewashed walls. Paintings of two large, red penises flanked the central window on the front wall. "The jewels in the heart of the lotus," Dasho liked to call these rustic phalluses. And indeed, most of the peasants of Jibesa related better to these symbolic assurances of good luck and fertility than to the flaming jewels, lotus blossoms, and other more sublime elements of Buddhist symbolism. Dasho's city neighbors would have considered him a rube if he had painted penises on the large, new house he had recently built for himself overlooking Thimphu, but still he had always liked the custom.

Dasho paused at the entrance to the kitchen room to let his eyes adjust to the dim light inside. The pungent smell of pine wood smoke instantly brought memories of his childhood. A dim form bowed to him, greeting, "Kuzu-zampo la Dasho." Without needing to see who it was, he answered, "Kuzamo, Zangmo" to his sister-in-law's familiar voice. He unbelted his sword and she hung it on a peg on the wall. Jigme led him over to the floor mats by the far end, where the smoke from the kitchen fire had not blackened the wall as badly, and they sat while Zangmo served them salty buttered tea and *zow*, a roasted puffed rice kernel snack. Dasho pulled his pouch of betel nut from his gho pocket and offered some to Jigme. Preparation of the *doma* quids was all part of the little social ceremony of betel chewing. Dasho spread white lime paste from his silver pillbox onto the betel leaf and then rolled a quarter nut into the quid. They chatted and savored the warm buzz, and now and then spat blood-red mouthfuls of formaldehyde-smelling juice and pulp into their little bowls, while the drizzly afternoon light faded outside.

After some time, Jigme asked, "So how long will you stay with us, Tshering?"

"Through Monday anyway." Then Dasho added, or maybe let slip because of the doma, "or, maybe I'll end up staying forever."

"Um, I don't understand," Jigme said after a moment. "Of course you can stay as long as you want, but . . . what exactly do you mean?".

Dasho waved his hand. "No, forget that. I'll go back to Thimphu on Monday morning." He paused for a moment wondering whether he should let his own problems intrude on the family's celebration. "Look, Jigme," he finally said, "I suppose that I should tell you. Kindly keep this between you and me for now, but I'm on administrative suspension, until the civil service commission decides what to do with me."

"You . . . they . . . you're no longer working as the city manager?" Jigme stammered.

16

"Well, officially I still am, but right now I am on . . . sort of a leave."

Jigme stared into his tea bowl to avoid meeting his brother's eyes. "Oh, I'm sorry. Um . . . excuse me for asking, . . . but why?"

"Why?" answered Dasho, "Because I tried to do my job and stepped on the toes of the wrong people, of the big shots, that's why." He saw his brother's embarrassment at having raised the awkward conversation, so decided to let it drop. "I don't want to talk about that now, though."

"I'm sorry," whispered Jigme.

Dasho spat into his bowl. "Yes, well, when you work for the government, you expect this sort of thing some fine day. I'm not going to let it spoil my weekend here. I'll tell the family when it's all done and settled, whichever way it turns out."

"Yes of course, Dasho."

A girl appeared and filled their tea bowls.

"Who is she?" Dasho asked Jigme. "I've never seen her here before."

"She's a relative of Zangmo's who is living with us now. She doesn't hear so well, but she's a good worker."

"Who are her parents?"

"Cousins of Zangmo. From Chapcha village. I don't think you know them. Her name is Tshering Denka, but everyone calls her Sonam."

"Why Sonam?"

Jigme took a sip of his tea. "They say that she is the reincarnation of a farmer from Chapcha who was named Sonam."

Dasho chuckled. "Why do they think that ?"

"They say she looks like him. He died about a year before she was born. He had killed another man once, in a fight. It was an accident; they both were drunk. The villagers think that it was his karma to be reincarnated as a deaf girl."

17

After living most of his adult life in towns and among educated government officials, Dasho no longer believed in such direct manifestations of reincarnation. Like the good-luck penises, the folk beliefs seemed like quaint, but slightly embarrassing, vestiges of simpler times. Nevertheless, he did believe, in a somewhat more general sense, in reincarnation and the law of karma. When he thought about the vicissitudes of his own career, he sensed that karma was running its relentless course on him. Dasho was born in Jibesa in 1943, two decades before the first road was built into Bhutan and the first Mahindra army jeeps rattled up it from India. A lama had given him the name Phub Dorji as an infant, but later in life he changed it to Tshering Tashi. Back then of course there were no government schools or basic health clinics in Jibesa or anywhere else in the country. Children learned what they had to know by helping their parents on the farm. Those who got sick or injured were healed by their grandparents' herbal remedies and by the village monks' pujas, or not at all. When the previous king ascended the throne in 1952, he decided that Bhutan must educate its young people if it ever hoped to join the developed world. A few years later, one of the king's retainers, a Jibesa man, identified eleven year-old Phub Dorji as a promising lad and he was sent to study in a mission school in Kalimpong. Although at first he was sad and missed his happy life of tending cows and playing with his friends, as it turned out, once he got used to being a student in India, he liked it and did very well.

After he passed-out from the school, he joined the Royal Bhutan Army and over the years rose to the rank of major. In 1985 he resigned and joined the civil service, and had been an administrator in one or another department of the Royal Government since. It seemed to him that the government had bounced him from one posting to another, always thankless ones, where an administrator who knew the necessity of discipline was needed to shake out inefficiency and laziness, where someone without particularly important family connections could take flak for making unpopular decisions and then be moved on to another post. In total, he had had six postings since he left the army, and three had been within the last four years. He had worked in Immigration and Census, the Finance Ministry, then had served as a district administrator, then as the Director of the Department of Public Works—none of which he had been trained for or particularly qualified for—and it had frustrated him that he had never had enough time to really settle into a posting before being transferred.

At times of frustration during his career, especially so during the last unsettling few years, he thought about karma; how violence, anger, and other negative thoughts and deeds in his life or past lives inevitably led to negative consequences. At one point in the mid 1970s, after a string of bad luck culminating in a fatal traffic accident involving some young recruits under his command, he changed his name to try to wipe his slate clean. He chose Tshering—meaning "long life" and Tashi—meaning "auspicious." A prosperous long life, he hoped. Old timers in the villages believed that by changing one's name, a person could elude bad demons which plagued him. Dasho did not believe in demons, but psychologically, it gave him confidence and a sense of starting fresh; and, indeed, his luck did seem to improve for a time afterward. As he grew older, he more and more made it a point to do acts of merit—donating to monasteries, sponsoring pujas, or doing whatever he could to help fire victims or the poor in Thimphu—to try to offset his own karma.

His Majesty the King conferred the title "Dasho" on him in 1991, after he was transferred from his posting as district administrator in Chirang. Dasho always said that his tenure in Chirang was the most difficult and nasty eighteen months of his career. At that time, some rabble rousers among the ethic Nepalese families in Chirang and other southern districts were protesting against the citizenship and immigration laws, and demonstration marches had escalated into decapitating policemen and burning down government schools and health clinics. Dasho kept control in Chirang District during his year and a half there, and when he left the situation was much calmer. Being awarded the title of "Dasho," with its prestige and its right to wear a sword and red scarf, was honorable compensation for that nasty period as DA, but he was sure glad when it had ended.

His present posting, as city manager of Thimphu, was his favorite. He found he could run the city staff more or less like an army regiment and direct their continuous "battles" with garbage pickup, water supply, stray dogs and livestock, street hawkers, and the rest of it. There were clear rules about sanitation, building permits, street setbacks, keeping livestock, and the like, which he tried to enforce to the letter. The trouble was, unlike in the army, vested interests from wealthy and powerful families were not about to take orders from him, and so his attempts to clean up the city were often frustrated. In the face of these frustrations, he liked to come back to his village and for a short time live its simple life without telephones or electricity, and where the farmers proudly looked up to him as Dasho, their benefactor, the village boy who made good.

Dasho lay under a warm blanket on a mattress in Jigme's main room. He listened to the peaceful breathing from the dim forms of the other family members huddled on the floor around him. It was still well before dawn, but he could not fall back asleep. He and Jigme had stayed up late drinking *ara*, homemade grain liquor, and he had had to get up a while ago to pick his way among the sleeping bodies out to the latrine. Now he lay awake listening: far-off bird chirping and rooster crowing drifting up from outside, and soft snoring around him. He felt Choeki, warm and soft, next to him. Choeki was a youngish widow, another cousin of some sort of Zangmo. Arrangements were always made for her to spend the night with Dasho when he came to Jibesa without his wife. At first she had been shy, but in the last few years had gotten more confident, teasing Dasho and telling him jokes. He always brought her something from the shops in Thimphu or a little money when he visited. Then there was *Ama* Deki, Zangmo's old mother. Dasho had heard her get up some time ago and go into the house's shrine room. He listened to her voice now through the wall, softly mumbling her morning prayers. Jibesa regarded Ama Deki as somewhat of a holy woman, and she was often asked to say prayers for driving away sickness from people and livestock. Around the house she helped out in whatever chores she was still able to do. But mostly she spent her days spinning her prayer wheel and mumbling prayers, counting off each set of one hundred and eight on her rosary.

When Dasho opened his eyes again dawn light was filtering between the window shutter gaps. Sleepers were beginning to stir under the blankets. He quietly gathered up his clothes and tiptoed to the kitchen room to dress. The thought came to him that he had not seen a sunrise in a long time, so he put his down vest on over his gho and creaked his stiff knees up to a terraced field above the house. From there, he gazed down over the houses of Jibesa, the freshly plowed potato and wheat fields that filled the bowl of the mountain valley, and across the main river valley to the next mountain range beyond. Yesterday's overcast and drizzle had cleared, but the lower river valley still hid under a blanket of puffy clouds. The cloudtops' daybreak pink gradually bleached away in the sun rays that began cresting the mountain ridge above him. Away to the west the moon was fading into clear blue sky. Wood smoke drifted up from the cook shed, where the hired help already had a pot of water boiling. The smell made him hungry, so he picked his way down from the terrace and joined them for a cup of sweet tea.

People streamed into Jibesa all morning. Families hiked in from more remote villages on the far sides of the mountain ridges. Others hitched or rode the bus from towns up and down the main river valley and got off at the base of the feeder road to walk up the last five kilometers. A few more families drove vehicles up from Thimphu. There had been no announcement of the puja on the radio, no newspaper bulletin or any other formal notice. But around the district word had spread that Lam Rinchen Tulku would be in Jibesa, and the people swarmed in for his blessing. Men wore their best ghos of colorful stripes or Hong Kong brocade. Women dug heirloom *kiras* from their family's trunks, ankle-length wrap dresses which were masterpieces of intricate color patterns woven in raw silk, and which they wore but once or twice a year. They carried thermos bottles of tea, baskets of rice, meat curries, and chilies; and spread their blankets on the temple's lawn to picnic and gossip and await the puja.

Lam Rinchen had been praying since dawn. A white cotton pavilion draped with yellow silk bunting had been set up outside the temple wall. Juniper boughs and fresh pine needles were spread under the tent and scattered around on the temple lawn. A few dozen young spruce trees cut from up on the mountain were planted around the perimeter of the lawn, each carefully stripped of its branches until only the top brush remained. Just after noon, when the spring sun had dried the ground and the picnickers were dozing in its warmth, a cacophonous blare of horns and cymbals erupted from inside the temple. Men hurried to set fire to small piles of juniper boughs, sending thick, sweet smoke into the eyes and lungs of everyone who sat downwind. Others shagged pebbles at the dogs scrounging for picnic scraps, driving them yelping from the temple area. The congregation gradually sat themselves into rows on the lawn: a man with a switch swatted excited boys who would not sit still. The sponsors of the puja—wealthier Jibesa farmers as well as city people who had driven up from the capital—sat in the front row. As the highest-ranking guest (and a big contributor), Dasho took his spot front and center. Several villagers started to stand as he walked to his place, but he waved for them to stay seated.

The clanging of cymbals, booming of the long horns, and jangling drone of the temple oboes grew louder. All eyes watched as the lama's procession emerged from the temple door. Children and adults chattered and laughed excitedly as the monks filed into the pavilion and sat on the ground in rows flanking a center dais. At the end of the procession came Lam Rinchen himself, dressed in a red miter and the orange shawl of his rank. Without any more ceremony he settled himself on the dais, took his lap dog from this attendant, and began reading aloud from the book of scriptures set out before him. A senior monk led the others in their accompaniment of the lama's recitation, clanging small cymbals to beat the rhythm of the chanting. Two monks picked up the beat on bright red temple drums, which they held upright from the ground on long handles. The chanting voices rose and fell, rose and fell like the perpetual respiration of humanity's lungs; trailing off into a sustained, growling sigh at the end of each verse, until resuscitated again by the primordial blare of the orchestra. Through it all, Lama Rinchen's Pekinese sat on the dais and gazed out at the congregation, chuffing through its underbite as if disapproving that the villagers were chatting and not paying much attention.

At intervals, the performance was punctuated with blessings of blue cords, red ribbons, and straws, which were then distributed among the villagers. Parents helped children tie the cords around their wrists and the ribbons around their heads. Knotted by the monks and blessed by

23

Lam Rinchen, they were charms for warding off evil. Only the monks were trained to understand Lama Rinchen's scriptures; for most of the congregation, the knotted wrist cords and ribbons were the main reason for coming. If many of the people tied them on the wrong way or missed cues to respond to the rituals, so did even some of the novice monks, and it was a cause for laughter, not embarrassment. After two hours, the lama abruptly closed the scripture and his attendant led him through the crowd, sprinkling water that he had blessed. The people prostrated themselves, touching their foreheads to the ground as the holy man passed, knowing that evil and misfortune had been purged and that health and abundant harvests were ensured for the coming year. Behind the lama came a monk with a collection bag, and the people were happy to gain religious merit by giving whatever they could afford.

The procession of monks returned to the temple and the crowd gradually broke up and drifted off, some to their houses in Jibesa or nearby villages, some down the feeder road to the highway and a long hitch or bus ride back home. The lama's Pekinese, which had been neglected at the end of the puja, was standing alone and quivering, being sniffed by three village mutts. Some boys came to its rescue, yelling "Chi" and winging pebbles at the local dogs, who bolted yelping across a field. Several villagers greeted Dasho as he walked from the temple's lawn, wishing him well. "Yes, yes," Dasho said, smiling. His troubles seemed far away as he walked up the hill to Jigme's house in the spring afternoon sunshine.

Dasho sat on the ground and rested against the tall stack of pine needles at the edge of the barn yard. Jibesa farmers collected basketsfull of pine needles from the forest and stored them for bedding for their livestock. He sat on the sunny side, out of the breeze, enjoying a cigarette while he waited until supper. The odor of manure wafting from

24

a sun-warmed pile near the barn door reminded him of his childhood there, and he sighed. He saw Sonam, the house girl, emerge from the barn with a basket load of manure and dump it onto the pile. It was a spring custom for farm woman and children to clean the barn and pack the winter's worth of manure out to fertilize the fields. Sonam noticed Dasho watching her and giggled. A pretty girl, he thought to himself, but she'll never do better in her life than be a peasant wife. Perhaps the villagers' belief, that this child's being born a girl and partially deaf was the karmic result of her previous incarnation's bad deeds, was right after all, he mused. How could you ever disprove it?

His train of thought shifted to his experience as DA during the disturbances in Chirang. His military training and experience had served him well there. He had not hesitated to crack down on the agitators and their collaborators when he had to, and had effectively used the militia and police units that were assigned to him. He certainly had not enjoyed ordering the arrests of demonstrators, the beatings and jailings, and the burning of farm houses. Personally he had no antipathy against the ethnic Nepali Bhutanese people who lived in the south, and the hardship which the violence and disruption caused them genuinely saddened him. But as far as he was concerned, the agitation was treason, and he did not let his sympathies hinder him from doing his duty to protect His Majesty and the nation.

But the fact was, his actions had caused people to suffer. And somehow, some time, the negative reaction would manifest itself. Perhaps the reaction was this present mess with the civil service commission. Or perhaps not, and he had escaped it for the time being by buying time with acts of merit. But he sensed that , as with Sonam the house girl, eventually the debt would be repaid. He stroked his mustache and flicked a cigarette ash off his gho, then leaned back against the warm pile and tried to regain his former contented mood. But the nostalgic spell had dissolved. He sighed and watched Sonam carry another basket from the barn.

Jigme saw Dasho sitting by the stack of animal bedding, distractedly picking pine needles from his clothes. "Anything wrong?" he asked.

"Ah, Jigme." Dasho beckoned him to sit down. "No, nothing is wrong." They sat for a while in silence in the late afternoon sun.

"I saw Lam Rinchen leaving in a big car with some city people a little while ago," Jigme said.

"Yes. In that blue government Land Cruiser. That was his niece and some of her children. I think you saw them at the puja, no? They will drive Lam Rinchen back to his monastery tomorrow." He paused for a moment, then added, "You know, her husband is the head of the civil service commission."

"Are all the lamas and dashos related to each other?"

Dasho laughed at his brother's innocence. "No, no. But you've got the right idea." He paused for a moment, then added. "Since you asked, here is another connection: her cousin—not on Lam Rinchen's side but on her father's side—owns one of the largest contracting companies in Bhutan. There were some bad feelings between him and me back when I was the PWD director and helped Jibesa's little contracting company build the feeder road to the village. He was counting on being able to use the PWD payloader that I dispatched here on one of his own projects that year and ended up falling several months behind schedule because he couldn't use it."

"Are you still on bad terms?"

"No, no. I made it up to him by approving his cost overruns on his project. So we are back on good terms now."

"That's good." Jigme picked a few pebbles from the dirt and lobbed them out into the kitchen garden plot. After a minute, he said, "Excuse me, brother, it is impolite to ask, but I'd like to know . . . "

"Sure, Jigme. What is it?"

He looked at the ground and said, "Just what exactly are the charges against you . . . if I may ask?"

Dasho looked Jigme in the face and frowned for a moment, then said, "O.K., I'll tell you. It seems that a few too many shopkeepers and hotel owners with high connections did not appreciate the fines I issued when they dumped their garbage in the drains and back lots. A few too many big shot property owners did not like being ordered to tear down their unpermitted additions to their houses, or their encroachments on government land. And now they have convinced the civil service commission to suspend me so that they can try to get the government to appoint a more compliant city manager." He lit a cigarette, took a drag, and continued in an angry tone. "The specific charges are 'misappropriation of government property and abuse of position.' They are both bullshit, Jigme. They're the kind of nonsense they use when they just want to get rid of someone. I tell you, in Thimphu there is a set of people with high connections—relatives and friends of the royal family and other big shots—who act like they own the place. And they accuse *me* of abuse of position when I stop them from building on government land, or issue a few fines for the most blatant violations. And *I* get charged with misappropriating government property when I take a small fraction of the perks that they help themselves to. It's completely unfair. I could tell you some whoppers, Jigme: logging contracts, electricity and irrigation projects that benefit their country estates, kickbacks from the Japanese for the telephone system contracts. And they want to sack me for taking a few perks."

Jigme just nodded, embarrassed that his brother was upset. "I'm sorry Tshering," he whispered.

"Don't be sorry," Dasho said. "I'm not going to be ashamed if I get sacked. To hell with them. You know, if I do get sacked, I've been thinking about going into business exporting Bhutanese textiles. It might be good for me to do something other than government service for a change."

"You won't get sacked," Jigme mumbled. "We'll say prayers for you."

The day after the puja remained warm and sunny, and picnics sprouted around the village. The neighbors built a camp fire on a terraced field above the temple and invited several families to join them. Jigme told his hired help to carry down baskets of rice and pork and vegetables and to help with the cooking. By midmorning, some boys started a game of *kuru*, in which each team threw home-made darts at small wooden targets set at either end of the field. The game went on for hours, with girls, men, and even some of the mothers trying a few throws.

Dasho's driver, Dilip, came down to the picnic site with the cooks. Although he understood only a little of the Dzongkha language that the villagers spoke, he was more comfortable with them than hanging around the house with Dasho's brother's family. At one point in the morning, as they were cutting up potatoes and turnips for the pot, one of the men tossed a potato at him. Everyone laughed, and Dilip picked it up and tossed it at another. Soon the potato was flying around among them and they could not stop laughing. Finally it landed in the fire and no one was willing to kick it out and continue the game. When the laughter subsided, one of the cook boys turned to Dilip and asked in Nepali language, "how long have you been Dasho's driver?"

"Two, three years," he answered.

"We hear that Dasho has some trouble with the government. Do you know anything about it?"

Dilip waggled his head and said, "They say that Dasho stole cement from the government to build his new house."

"Is it true?"

Dilip shrugged. "He told me to pick up some bags of cement at one of the city's construction sites and drive them to his house, which I did. Six, seven bags. Not much."

"Ehh," said the other men, and some shook their heads. They all went back to cutting up chilies and pork and potatoes for the picnic meal, and no one said anything else for a while.

By midday, dozens of neighbors arrived with plastic jugs of ara liquor and *sinchang* barley beer, and helped themselves to the steaming vats of rice and pork fat and chili and cheese curry. Between helpings some men began a stone throwing game, sailing flat rocks discus-style at a target pit on a nearby unplowed field. Swarms of flies, resurrected by the sunshine, buzzed all around. Doma passed around among the adults, and their boozy smiles reddened with betel juice. Feasting, drinking, and sports went on throughout the afternoon. The hosts had carried a small couch and a low table out to the field for Dasho to sit at, as befitted his rank, but after a few cups of ara, and teary-eyed from the smoky fire, Dasho joined a group of older men on the ground at dice. Most of them he knew as strong youths or handsome young fathers when he was a young boy in Jibesa. Now they were stooped and wrinkled; some had goiters or cataracts, none still had all his teeth. They sat in a ring and bet old *paisa* and *chetrum* coins as each took a turn shaking the cup and slapping the dice down with a shout. The winners collected their coins, all laughed and took another drink, and the dice went to the next man in the ring. Dasho realized that he hadn't enjoyed himself as much in a long time. It crossed his mind briefly

29

that he was losing more than he won, and that this seemed to be his karma these days, but it did not spoil his fun.

Zangmo, Choki, and several of the neighbor women spent the afternoon singing songs and talking. When someone began singing a dance song, they staggered to their feet and danced the steps, shrieking gleefully when one or another stumbled, then collapsed back down into their circle in fits of laughter. Later in the afternoon, one woman sent her son back to the house to fetch her three-string village lute. The *dramnyen* music energized their singing, and they shouted for the children and men to join the dances. For a half hour or more all the picnickers danced to the old familiar songs; even Dasho joined them in their big, slow circle, shuffling the simple steps and swinging his arms and hands in graceful, sinuous curves. Eventually, chilly air blowing up from the river valley's shadows gradually broke up the circle, and people dropped away to gather their children and walk home to evening chores.

On Monday, after breakfast, Dilip carried Dasho's bags and sword down to the road head and loaded them into the Hilux. He and Dasho drove down the rutted feeder road to the highway in silence, and only spoke a few times on the drive back to the city. Dasho was thinking about some Swiss consultants he had made friends with back when he was the PWD Director, and how perhaps they could give him some business contacts for exporting textiles to Europe.

Vishwakarma Puja

After lunch, Bhakta drove the open bed Tata back to the city corporation's garage. He decided to cruise up Thimphu's main street and then double back, because it was more fun than taking the direct route along the bypass. There was always something to watch on Norzim Lam. This afternoon he had had to brake hard just past the police kiosk to avoid rear-ending a hilux, which had stopped in the road to let its passengers climb out. Bhakta had been waving to one of the young, white-gloved traffic cops whom he knew and hadn't noticed the hilux until the very last second. Naturally the usual crowd of unemployed young men and monks loafing in front of the cinema hall had erupted in laughter and cheers at the near accident. Bhakta had smiled back and waved.

The Tata was the oldest of Thimphu City Corporation's three working garbage pickup trucks. There was a fourth truck, but it had been off-road since June. Repeated calls to the supplier in Calcutta had not yet produced the spare part for its broken hydraulics. But that was the city's mechanic's responsibility, not Bhakta's. Bhakta's usual morning route went along Norzim Lam through the upper bazaar, where most of the shops and hotels were. He would drive slowly, stopping every ten meters or so and blasting the truck's air horn to signal shop keepers and hotel kitchen boys to bring out their garbage bins. Bhakta had two helpers, Bhim Bahadur and Pasang. They stood in the truck's open bed, and when the shop keepers handed their bins up, they emptied them and handed them back down. Then they thumped on the roof and Bhakta would drive on a bit further and blast the horn again. He liked the horn noise: it made people jump if they did not expect it. Whenever the truck's bed became more or less full of garbage, Bhakta would drive up to the landfill, where Bhim and Pasang let down the wood slat sides and shoveled it out. On most mornings, two trips to the landfill were enough to finish the upper bazaar.

In the afternoons, Bhakta's crew was supposed to collect garbage from whichever parts of the city had fallen behind schedule. Today they had been assigned to do catch-up in Mutithang, a neighborhood of expensive homes on the west slopes of the valley above town. On his second trip back from the landfill that morning, though, Bhakta had noticed that the truck's fuel gauge read nearly empty. He cut the engine and coasted most of the way back to town, and decided that it would probably be futile to try to refuel that afternoon. The section officer who normally signed the diesel vouchers and recorded the amount in the fuel ledger was on leave from work today, and the engineer, who could also sign vouchers, might not be at the office. The garage caretaker, of course, was not allowed to pump fuel without a signed voucher. So, there was nothing else to do but call it a day. Mutithang's garbage could always wait a few days, no problem. And besides, tomorrow was *chutti*, a holiday.

It was still only two o'clock. Since they were supposed to be on the job until four, Bhakta and Pasang and

Bhim Bahadur killed time by kicking a hacky sack around in the warm September sunshine. As usual, Bhakta wore the city corporation's blue coveralls with an old pair of cowboy boots and a stained Chicago Bulls cap. He had bought the boots and cap from a Bangladeshi clothing seller at Thimphu's weekend bazaar. He heard that American-style clothes like the cap and boots were donated to Bangladesh from the USA for flood disaster relief, and then resold in places like Thimphu's bazaar. It did not matter to him where they came from. He liked the fancy boots, and wearing the cap let him feel less self-conscious about his scarred scalp and face. He had been burned in an accident the previous winter and the cap somewhat masked the disfigurement. Also, he liked to think that the boots and cap gave him his own image: sort of a Tata diesel cowboy. He was proud to be a truck driver. True, driving garbage to the landfill was not the most prestigious job in the world, but he could do worse. At least he never had to touch the garbage: that was his two helpers' job. He liked driving the garbage truck for the city and was grateful to the gods for having any job at all.

By three o'clock all the other city corporation work crews had finished for the day and drifted back to the garage. Today was pay day and the workers assembled an hour early to get their pay. The other truck drivers, Karchung, Pradhan, Phuntsho, and Man Bahadur, stood together and talked. Man Bahadur, who drove the newer of the city's two dump trucks, was the senior driver at city corporation. He always drove for construction and maintenance work, water supply, that sort of thing; he never did garbage pickup. Bhakta admired him. He was handsome and confident and honest. The section officers often asked Man Bahadur for his advice in work crew scheduling and other matters. Last year, Bhakta used to join in with the other drivers' conversations. But now they usually ignored him, or at best called him "Burn Man" when they had to

33

talk shop with him. These days he felt more comfortable with the company of Bhim and Pasang.

The street sweeping and drain clearing crews were also waiting to get paid. The workers on these crews were mostly women, the wives of many of the drivers and helpers. Each crew also had a few either very young or not-very-capable men, and one older fellow, who had earned enough seniority over the years to be a foreman. The sweepers, like most of the other workers, were uneducated villagers from western and southern Bhutan, who for various reasons had left their villages to do wage work in the capital. Bhakta's wife, Chini Maya, was a street sweeper. At the garage the sweeper crews mostly kept to themselves, chatting, smoking cheap, Indian cigarettes called *bidis*, and keeping an eye on their babies and toddlers, whom they brought to their work sites each day. They carried the babies in large, colorful shawls, which they draped under the baby's bottom, then looped over their shoulders and tied behind the back. Strapped on her back, it was easy for Chini Maya to keep track of her daughter Subhi while she swept the streets. Toddlers, though, could be difficult when they fussed or wandered, so the mothers left those older than two or three at home.

Finally, at 3:30, the engineer showed up with his briefcase full of cash. He called roll, starting with the drivers, then helpers, then sweepers. As each worker came forward to get his or her wad of bills, a section officer recorded his or her name and the amount in neat handwriting in the pay ledger. The worker signed next to his name, or inked her thumb on the ink pad and made a thumb print if she did not know how to write. Drivers like Bhakta usually made 1,800 rupees a month. Really though their pay was based on sixty rupees a day. If they showed up for work each day Monday through Saturday, the city corporation paid them for their day off on Sunday too. If not, they were paid only for the days they worked. So if he showed up

34

regularly, Bhakta cleared Rs. 1,800 a month. The helpers, of course, earned less, Rs. 1,500 a month; the sweepers, Rs. 1,200.

On paydays the drivers and helpers usually stopped at the bars in town for a few pegs of Bhutan Mist whiskey before going home. Bhakta used to join them, but since the fire last winter he had been trying to quit drinking. Besides, since the fire, the drivers generally ignored him, so bar hopping with them was no fun any more. The women, of course, always wanted to take their babies straight home and start cooking their families' suppers. Chini Maya, Man Bahadur's wife Sita, Karchung's wife, and the others who lived at Bhakta's camp had already lifted their children into the bed of his Tata and were impatient to go. Chini whistled at Bhakta to get moving. These days, and especially on payday when the others went drinking, he was sort of the shuttle bus driver for his camp. He did not mind; in fact it made him feel good to be useful. He kicked the hacky sack back and forth with Bhim and Pasang a few more times (to show that Chini could not order him around), then bowed to the ladies and started the truck for home.

The workers' camp where Bhakta and Chini Maya lived was across the river and upstream from Thimphu. Its seventeen huts were clustered in the bottom and up the sides of a little draw which led off the main road. The city corporation had set up this camp after its bigger camp site closer to the garage had been taken over for a government project. The civil servant and shop owner families living in the vicinity of the old camp, who had grumbled for years about the unattractive huts and the unsupervised Hindu children running around during the day, were relieved when the government finally condemned the land. The huts in the new camp were tidier than the old ones: identical two-room buildings of bamboo mat walls and corrugated galvanized steel sheet roofs over sturdy lumber

35

frames. The city installed a water tap, which was fed from the creek at the top of the draw, and a latrine at the bottom, where the creek flowed into the river. The neighbors at the old site used to complain that the children frequently did not use the latrine. Across the river at the new site, such lapses in sanitation bothered no one.

Although further from town, all in all it was a fairly pleasant location. It was quiet, it caught the warm afternoon sunshine for a half hour after Mutithang had slipped into the mountain's shadow, and there was plenty of space for the worker's cattle to graze on the forested slopes above the water supply intake. For a while, after the men had rigged up a tap from the power lines along the river, the camp even had electricity. But after the fire the previous winter, the Power Department discovered the unauthorized connections and removed them. One of these days the men planned to hook up a new tap and run the cable down the utility pole and through the culvert under the road so it would not be so noticeable. But they had to wait for the right time to do it, such as early in the morning on a government holiday, so as not to get caught.

Children and dogs came running when the Tata lumbered into camp. Several chickens scattered squawking ahead of them. As the women began to climb down from the bed, Bhakta's four-year old son Pravis ran to the cab and shouted, "Up! Up!" Bhakta lifted him into the cab and hugged him, but the boy was less interested in his dad than in standing on the seat, turning the wheel, and making truck noises. Pravis stayed at the camp during the day, watched over, more or less, by Didi. Didi was the older sister of one of the other women on Chini Maya's sweeper crew. Not having a paying job, she stayed at the camp all day and generally kept an eye on the young children while their parents were at work. There were a few times when Pravis was really sick—a chest infection once, a bad ear infection another time—when Chini Maya skipped work

36

and took him to the hospital. At Thimphu's hospital, treatment and medicines were free, but patients had to wait in line for most of the day to get them. Actually, a day at the hospital was a nice break from work every once and a while. Chini Maya had two distant relatives on the staff—the floor sweeper at the outpatient department and a technician at the lab—so she could visit with them while she waited. If they were not around she could always learn the latest gossip from some of the other mothers in the waiting line. But a day at the hospital meant a day's pay lost, so if it was only diarrhea or a fever, Chini brought Pravis or Subhi to Didi's hut and asked her to care for them during the day. She always returned the favor in some way.

When Bhakta came into his hut with Pravis, Chini Maya already had the cooking fire started. She cooked on a clay-earth stove built on the floor of the kitchen room, feeding sticks, wood scraps, and sawdust into the hole in its side. Her pans fit over two smaller holes in the top of the stove; smoke curled to the corrugated steel roofing sheets and seeped out the gaps above the walls. Firewood was a constant concern of the camp workers. On Sunday afternoons, the women combed the mountainside above the camp for dead sticks. Every month the men drove a truck to the sawmill at the south side of town and loaded it with saw scraps and saw dust. The mill's foreman was a friend of Man Bahadur's and he charged them only fifty rupees a truck load.

"You'll have to cut some log wood for the winter Bhakta," Chini Maya called as he passed her.

He went into the main room and tucked his pay money under the mattress on the bed platform. "Yes. Maybe we will go next Sunday. Not tomorrow, it's a holiday." Each fall Bhakta and some of the younger men felled pines in the forest above the camp and skidded them down for firewood. Proximity to the forest for firewood poaching was another advantage of the new camp site over the old

37

one in town. Cutting trees in the forest was illegal, so they had to be careful about how they did it. Unfortunately, during the past few summers the rain had eroded their skid trails into deep gullies. The gullies were becoming increasingly conspicuous to the forestry office across the valley, and government forestry guards had begun patrolling the slopes. To avoid being caught and fined, the men had to cut at dawn or dusk, and even then, post a lookout.

Bhakta sat on the bed platform in the main room and held baby Subhi while Chini Maya cooked. Pencil beams of the setting sun were streaming through several small holes where the newspaper and thin plaster lining of the bamboo mat walls had deteriorated. He made a mental note to re-plaster the walls some weekend before the winter set in. Some of the beams fell on the rickety table with half-burned incense sticks and a glass jar of wilted marigolds that made up their household shrine. In the shadow above the table was a color post card showing Shree Ganesh, the chubby, elephant-headed god of good fortune, with a handsome couple and two happy children sitting at his feet. Of all the gods, Bhakta felt he could relate best with Ganesh. His images were inevitably unthreatening: smiling, childlike, and forgiving. Bhakta sang a funny old song to Subhi and she smiled at him and cooed *"baabaa."* Pravis kept running from the kitchen room and leaping onto the bed platform behind his father.

"Don't be a naughty boy!" shouted Chini Maya, after about his fifth leap. "Bhakta, don't let him run wild."

He sighed at her cutting tone. "Enough, Pravis, you're bothering *aamaa*," he said. "Such a naughty boy," he added with a wink. After a moment he set the baby down and took the boy's hand. "Here *bhai*, help me fill the lantern," he said. He took a lantern from a nail in a rafter and set it on the bed platform. Pravis scuttled to the corner of the platform and stared nervously while Bhakta got the jug of kerosene from the kitchen and filled the lantern.

"Don't be afraid, Pravis, it won't start a fire," soothed Bhakta, as he hung the lantern back on its nail.

Chini Maya brought a plate of chappatis and pots of potato curry and rice from the kitchen and set them on the platform. She served her husband and Pravis, then filled her own plate. Bhakta tried to help Pravis eat, but the boy seemed intent on fussing and tearing his chappati into little bits, so he gave up and ate his own meal heartily. Chini Maya glanced at them a time or two, but said nothing until Pravis dropped a handful of rice onto the platform. She glared at Bhakta and said, "Bhakta, can't you see he's spilling it? Make him eat. Don't let him play with the food." He was about to retort that she should feed Pravis herself, but seeing that she was already hand-feeding Subhi, picked the boy up and set him in his lap. "Here Pravis, eat with your baabaa," he said, and rolled some curry into a chappati for him. He and Chini ate in silence for several more minutes, avoiding each other's eyes. Eventually Chini Maya finished and took the plates and pots to the kitchen to wash. The children never seem to eat much, Bhakta thought. He wondered whether Chini nursed Subhi enough. They were pretty healthy though, thank the gods, so they must be getting what they need.

"Do you remember that Suresh's bus comes in at around noon tomorrow?" she called from the kitchen.

"*Hunchha.*"

"You're going to meet him at the bus station, aren't you?"

"Um, I planned to go to the garage early tomorrow to set up for the *puja.* I figure that Suresh can walk to our house by himself, then join us at the puja." Chini Maya did not respond. He knew by her silence, though, that she disapproved of this plan.

"Aamaa, aamaa I want some water," said Pravis, jumping off the bed and scooting into the kitchen.

"Here, bhai, come sit by me and let mother work," called Bhakta. He filled a cup from the water bucket in the kitchen.

Chini Maya kept her back to him at the wash tub, so he led Pravis back to the main room. After an uncomfortably long pause, she said, "Bhakta, you haven't seen Suresh in two years."

"He knows how to find us. He's been here before. I can't go to the bus station at noon. They need me to help set up for the puja."

"He's your little brother, Bhakta. You can't just let him get off the bus with no one to greet him."

"He knows that he is welcome here. He won't feel bad if I don't meet him."

"Well, I'll go and meet him then." She called out to Pravis in a more cheerful sounding voice, "Bhai! Do you want to go with me tomorrow to meet Uncle Suresh?"

Pravis jumped up from the floor and ran back into the kitchen to his mother. "Yeah! Uncle!"

His big, black eyes, so bright and excited, made her laugh quietly. "Do you like uncle?" she asked, hugging him.

"Hunchha!"

"At least *we* do."

Bhakta scowled. Every other day or so they had some sort of argument like this. It made him sad. The arguments were always so petty. "Pravis," he called out, "you don't even remember Uncle Suresh, do you?"

"Yes I do."

Night had fallen and Bhakta was lighting the lantern when Chini Maya finished in the kitchen. "Bhakta, I'm going over to visit with Sita," she said as she got her shawl from a box under the platform. "Would you put Subhi to bed, please?"

Bhakta waggled his head to indicate "O.K." The baby was already dozing on the platform next to him. After

40

Chini left, he set Subhi on the far corner of the mattress, snugged a blanket around her, and kissed her forehead. When he sat back down, Pravis came over and snuggled his head in his lap. "It was a busy day for you bhai, wasn't it?" he said.

Pravis yawned.

"And tomorrow will be another busy day. Vishwakarma Puja. It will be a lot of fun, won't it?"

The boy nodded.

"You're not a naughty boy, are you?"

Pravis was too sleepy to answer.

Bhakta stroked his sleeping son's head. The flickering amber light of the kerosene lantern made him feel sleepy too. He thought about how life had been easier before the fire. They had owned a kerosene cooking stove then and had an electric light. On many evenings he would sing along with Nepali song tapes on his cassette player and visit with the other men in the camp. On a Saturday night like this, he might have had some drinks with the other drivers and gone to the cinema hall to watch a Hindi movie. He rubbed the burn scar on his cheek. Now the drivers seldom even talked to him. And Chini Maya had changed too. The sort of petty arguments like this evening's were rare then and easily forgotten. They used to have a lot of fun just talking with each other. They did not talk as much now. He listened to the voices and the dogs barking outside as the men returned from the bars. Oh well, he thought, things are getting better again. Both he and Chini were making money. They would buy some hens next month and maybe in the winter he would get a new tape player. And thanks to Shree Ganesh and Laxmi and all the other gods they were all healthy and together.

Vishwakarma Puja is the Hindu festival that honors Shree Vishwakarma, who is a son of Lord Vishnu and the patron of mechanical things, of industry, of those who use

41

tools to earn their living. Shree Vishwakarma has pale blue skin, rides on an elephant, and holds a tool in each of his four hands. He protects the tools of those workers who honor him, and brings them good fortune. At his festival in September, a month or so before the great holidays of Dasain and Diwaali, Hindu workmen prepare the machines and equipment that they use in their jobs for his blessing. Tailors oil their sewing machines, mechanics clean their wrenches, construction bosses tune up and decorate the company's cement mixer and air compressor. And especially, drivers prepare their motor vehicles. Taxis, trucks, pay loaders, even motor scooters are washed and waxed, get new oil and filters, and are decorated with ribbons and tinsel and pictures of the god to seek his blessing for smooth running for the year ahead.

On Sunday morning, Chini Maya got up at dawn as usual, cooked breakfast, then took the week's laundry down to the river bank. Her friend Sita was already there, beating soapy clothes on the smooth river boulders and then rinsing them in the swift-running current. By mid-morning, several families' clothing would be draped over the riverside bushes to dry in the sun, looking like bright tropical blossoms from the neighborhoods across the valley. Sita filled Chini in on some gossip that Man Bahadur had picked up at the bars the previous evening, and they made plans for the day. They decided to go to the weekend market to shop for the week's vegetables and then go straight to the bus station. That way Chini's brother-in-law Suresh could help carry their shopping back to the camp. There would be food at the puja, so there was no need to cook lunch. Later in the afternoon they would spend a few hours collecting firewood. Their husbands would certainly be out carousing at the celebrations until late, so they agreed to have supper together at Sita's hut.

Bhakta left the camp and drove the Tata up the river road, past the crematorium to the turnoff to the old river ford. He edged the truck out onto the gravel bank and then parked it in the shallow current. With a rag and some of Chini Maya's laundry soap he washed a year's worth of dust and grease off the truck body, then rinsed it all over with several buckets of water. The truck's orange paint shined when he pulled into city corporation's lot an hour later. Tshering, the garage caretaker, had already carried out boxes of decorations and the brightly painted, knee-high ceramic statue of Shree Vishwakarma and his elephant, which city corporation had ordered from sculptors down in Phuntsholing a few months before. Bhakta felt a bit guilty that, because of his tough circumstances, he had only been able to donate twenty rupees for the statue donation drive this year. He chatted with Tshering for an hour or so until a few other workers arrived, then they set about rigging up a pavilion for the ceremony. They built a frame of scrap lumber, spread a plastic tarp over the top, and decorated it with a string of blinking colored lights, pine boughs, ribbons, and balloons. They let down the sides of a trailer and wheeled it under the pavilion for an altar. In the center they set up the statue and surrounded it with wrenches, spanners, garlands of marigolds, oil filters, incense, hydraulic jacks, and a plate for cash offerings.

Bhakta next began to painstakingly decorate his truck. He lined the windshield with tinsel garlands, taped balloons to the sides, and wove red and blue ribbons across the radiator grill. Eventually, more workers and their families drifted in. The driver Pradhan brought a boom box and some of the latest Hindi rap tapes. Men and children began decorating the pay-loader, dump trucks and the other city vehicles. More people arrived and the boom box was turned up. Boys and girls grabbed plastic garlands and ribbons and tied them helter skelter onto the trucks. Some threw tinsel around the dashboards and taped pictures of Vishwakarma on the windshields. Others stuck smoldering

43

incense sticks under windshield wipers and painted good-luck swastikas on the hoods. With shrieks of laughter, more balloons were popped than taped to the trucks. Bhakta's careful decoration scheme on his Tata began looking wilder and wilder as more marigold garlands and tinsel and balloons were taped on, but he did not mind. The children and their antics and the shrieks and the loud music made him excited and happy.

By one o'clock, nearly all the families were there. Chini Maya had arrived with Suresh and Pravis and Subhi. The *pandit*, the learned man who knew the prayers for such festivals, also had come. Many children from neighborhood Buddhist families heard the loud music, had come to the garage to join the fun, and were running around with the workers' children, popping balloons and shrieking. The city engineer, the deputy director, and a few other "sirs" from the office had arrived and taken seats of honor under the pavilion. Bhakta and the caretaker handed out beers and sodas, sticky sweet *julabis*, hot samosas, and paper plates of spicy peanut and fried noodle snack. As more children clamoured around and the samosas ran out, Bhakta and Tshering filled a wash basin with sliced apples, bananas and sugar cane and handed them out on squares of newspaper.

In the midst of all the eating and drinking and loud music and running children, the pandit quietly drew the appropriate symbols on the ground in colored powders, lit some incense, and said the required prayers. He then took a bowl of red paint and daubed a *tika* mark on the hood of each vehicle with his finger. Bhakta and some of the others mixed bowls of paint and gleefully daubed good luck tika spots on every forehead within reach. As at a rollicking snowball fight, tika-ing became infectuous: sirs, drivers, sweepers, men, women, children, Hindus, Buddhists, laughed and tika-ed each other's brow. Even the dogs got

44

tika-ed, which made the children shriek louder. Bhakta forgot his self-consciousness about his scars; he could not stop laughing, and everyone laughed with him. The women chatted happily and ate, the men drank and danced to the music, the children ran all over and laughed and teased the barking dogs. Bhakta noticed how lovely Chini Maya looked when she laughed. It was a relief to see her happiness; he felt optimistic that her resentment would sooner or later run its course.

By mid afternoon the little ones were sleepy and their mothers walked them back across the river to the camp. Most of the men stayed to visit the other Vishwakarma Puja parties that were being held around the city. They climbed into the bed of a dump truck, those already on board pulling up those below. Bhakta's brother Suresh was hauled up, but when Bhakta raised his hand for a lift, no one grabbed it. The pause was only for a second or two, but long enough for his heart to sink. Then it was Man Bahadur who reached down and gave him his hand. "C'mon up ol' Burn Man," he said. Bhakta climbed in and smiled thinly back at Man Bahadur, relieved that the men's laughing and merriment continued as before, then joined Suresh in the corner of the truck. Karchung, the least drunk among them, climbed into the cab and started the engine. Diesel smoke belching, men singing and cheering, the boom box blaring, and tinsel garlands and balloons flapping, he ground the gears and lumbered out onto the road.

They soon found themselves in a parade of decorated vehicles driving the circuit of the parties around the city. First they visited the parties at the automobile repair workshops, one after another. Then to the Public Works garage, then to the sawmill; on and on, picking up more vehicles and passengers, and consuming more beer and snacks as they went. In the evening the parade ended up at a construction site for a new hotel. The Indian contractor

45

had really outdone himself, rigging up a generator and colored party lights and a sound system blasting Hindi movie
music. The celebration was still going strong; Bhakta was
primed to dance and drink all night. But Suresh was tired:
he had not slept since leaving Phuntsholing at six that
morning and asked Bhakta if he would mind going back
to the camp. "No problem," said Bhakta. And he meant it.
He was the happiest that he had been in many months and
nothing would spoil his mood.

Bhakta and Suresh left the party and followed unlit
footpaths through vacant lots down to the road along the
river. Bhakta sang one of the Hindi movie hits in his mind,
soaking up the merriment of the day, the cool darkness of
the evening, and the rushing sound of the river. He felt
foggy and sleepy from all the beer he had drunk during
the afternoon. They walked up stream towards the camp
in silence.

"It's been a long time since we've seen each other,
daju," Suresh said after some time. "I didn't meet you at
census this year."

Bhakta was surprised. "Didn't you know I was in
the hospital after the fire? I couldn't go to census. Chini
Maya said she told you."

"Of course I knew. Both Chini Maya and our cousin
M.P. Gurung told me about it. I'm just saying it's been a
long time since we've seen each other."

"Yes. Two years, I think."

They walked along, past a dark construction site. A
guard dog barked from inside the fence.

"You saw M.P.?" Bhakta asked.

"Yes, he was in Chirang the same day that I was to
register for the census. By the way, did you register at all
this year?"

"No. I was in the hospital. I couldn't. Chini Maya
went and she took my identification card. The deputy director at our office wrote a letter for me for the police and
district administrator. He said that was enough."

46

"They say you're supposed to go in person."

"The hospital wouldn't let me go. It wasn't my fault. The DD said that his letter was enough for the police. Don't you think that a letter was OK?"

"I suppose so."

"I don't want any trouble with the police."

"No. I'm sure the letter was enough, Bhakta."

They walked along the dark road, listening to the river. Bhakta had lost the tune in his head and could not pick it up again. The smell of smoke from wood stoves and cooking fires drifted down from the houses on the slopes to settle in the valley bottom. Far off they could still hear music from a Vishwakarma Puja party, fading in and out as the breeze changed. After some time, Bhakta asked, "Did you see our farm when you were in Chirang?"

"No. I haven't seen it since last year. The fields were overgrown with bushes and small trees even then. In a few more years it will all be back to jungle." Suresh paused a while. "You know, I heard from a guy in Siliguri that father and mother and Surjha are still at the Jhapa refugee camp. They . . ."

"Who'd you hear that from?" Bhakta cut in.

"He's a cousin, from mother's sister's husband's family. I'm sure you don't know him."

"Are they O.K.?"

"I guess. He really didn't know anything else."

"Ehh, *Bagwaan!*" sighed Bhakta. "I miss mother and father and our little sister." He sighed again and sniffed. His happy mood was gone and he felt like crying. Too much beer, he thought. "I miss our farm, too. It used to be so nice there. Not like this cold city."

"Yes, daju. What a disaster."

"Was that our karma, Suresh?"

"I don't know."

"I guess it was our karma."

47

They walked along. The lights of the bridge across the river to the workers' camp came into view.

"How do you like Phuntsholing?" Bhakta asked Suresh.

"*Raamrai chha.* I manage O.K. I like my job fixing scooters and I'm learning to repair truck engines. Megraj and Mangala don't seem to mind me staying with them."

"They are good cousins."

"Yes they are." He kicked a pebble out of the road. "You know, I was thinking of talking to some of the Thimphu workshops while I'm here to see if there might be a job. I think I'd rather live here than in Phuntsholing."

"The winters are freezing here, bhai. You can make more money, but it's also more expensive."

"Yeah, well, . . . You're doing O.K. here, though, aren't you? You've got your job and your two children. And no one hassles you, isn't it?"

Bhakta realized that it felt good to talk with his brother, and how much he missed talking like this with Man Bahadur and Chini Maya and the rest of his old friends. He took Suresh's hand and squeezed it gently. "Oh, our life here is good enough now. But when we first came here five years ago, we were miserable. You don't know how scared and lonely we were, Suresh. You were staying with Mangala and Megraj that winter when the army was arresting people and burning those houses in our village, but you must have heard how it was. Baabaa and aamaa got so scared by the DA's goons and their threats that they turned in their identification cards and left for Nepal. I would have gone too, but Chini Maya refused to go. It seemed too dangerous to stay at the village, bhai. We didn't know what would happen, whether we'd be arrested or robbed or whatever. So we came up here to Thimphu." He let go of his brother's hand and breathed in the cool air; Suresh didn't say anything. "But besides one of Chini's cousins who works at the hospital," Bhakta went on, "we had no relatives or friends here. She cried alot, which got me crying too."

"Pah."

"But life got better—making new friends, having the children, learning to drive trucks and getting this job." He paused. "I was lucky to get my job back, bhai."

"After the accident?"

"Yes." Bhakta paused for a moment, then added, "It was a stupid thing to do, bhai. I . . . I was drunk. But that was my karma too, wasn't it? That's what I am thinking anyway."

"I'm not blaming you, daju."

"I don't want to talk about it."

"Don't talk about it then. I'm not blaming you." He tried to change the subject. "How long have you been back working, anyway?"

"Only two months."

"You were out a half a year . . . pah! I didn't know."

"Yes. I was in the hospital for two months with the burns. Um, then, after I got out, I just sat around at our house. I sat around for three months before they hired me back. Just to teach me a lesson, you know?"

"Pah!"

"We lost everything . . . But things are getting better now."

"How did Chini Maya take it?"

"She doesn't really trust me any more; I'm not sure if she even likes me much now. And the other families . . . they hate me, I guess. I don't want them to hate me, Suresh. They're still my friends."

"They don't hate you, daju."

They walked across the bridge and turned towards the camp. Bhakta took his brother's hand again as they walked. "I'm glad you came to visit, bhai," he said, "I missed you."

"I'm glad to be here, daju."

49

On Monday morning the section officer came back from leave and signed a voucher for diesel for Bhakta's truck. Bhim and Pasang had been out drinking and singing at the parties late into the night, and were still in jolly moods as they collected the garbage bins from the upper bazaar. Bhakta had gone to bed in a melancholy mood after his talk with Suresh, but by the morning's first run up to the landfill, Bhim and Pasang's jokes and the shiny tinsel garlands on the truck had cheered him up. They all sang in the cab as he swung the truck around the tight curves on the narrow mountain road. He drove fast to give Bhim and Pasang a thrill. If there had been any oncoming traffic at the blind curves they would have collided for sure; but Vishwakarma's blessing was fresh, so Bhakta knew that the road would be clear. On the way back through the city before lunch break, Bhakta stopped at a shop and bought twenty five kilogram sacks of rice for himself and his neighbors in the camp. During the pay fall-in on Saturday afternoon he had offered to pick up the month's rice for the camp's families; Pradhan, Man Bahadur, and a few others had given him money for their orders. He was pleased with himself to be able to do them the favor.

Suresh had nothing else to do that day, so he joined Bhakta in the truck when they returned to the garage after lunch. They picked up Bhim and Pasang and drove up to Mutithang to finish up what they had missed on Saturday afternoon. That morning there had been several complaints from Mutithang residents: Mutithang's dogs and cows had been busy over the past three or four days, tipping over garbage bins, getting into the concrete collection pits, and strewing garbage around. The section officer had told Bhakta to be sure to finish that route today.

While Bhim and Pasang shoveled garbage from the concrete pits and sidewalks, Bhakta and Suresh sat in the cab and swapped memories from the time when they were boys on their family's farm in Chirang. Back then it was their job to tend the cattle, taking them out to the jungle to graze each morning and leading them back to the cow shed each evening. Those were fun, carefree days of wandering in the jungle and meadows, picking orchids and rhododendron blossoms and slinging stones at birds and monkeys. At times there was hard work on the farm, too, and sometimes not much to eat; but the memories of fun times were stronger and more vivid than those of bad ones. Before long Bhim told them that the truck was full. It was only two thirty; one more load would finish Mutithang up.

On the way back from the landfill they passed the garage and saw that some of the other crews were already hanging around at the lot. Although Vishwakarma Puja had officially been the previous day, there was still one final ceremony which had to be performed. The deputy director had instructed the section officers not to let the ceremony start until after work ended at four o'clock, but already half of the sweepers and two of the truck crews had assembled. Bhakta, Bhim, and Pasang decided that the rest of Mutithang's garbage could wait another day: Vishwakarma Puja came around only once a year.

Bhakta and three other men carefully lifted Shree Vishwakarma's statue from its altar and placed it into the Tata's open bed. The assembled workers all climbed in with the god, the men pulling up wives with babies tied to their backs. With the two SOs leading the way on a motor scooter, Bhakta drove the truck out of town, ribbons and tinsel garlands and now-deflated balloons flapping in the breeze. A high overcast had drifted in from the south and a few rain drops sprinkled the windshield. The riders chatting and singing in the back did not seem to notice. Tawny green rice, nearly ready to harvest, bowed in the breeze in the paddies along the valley bottom. Chili peppers were turning scarlet on the roofs of the farmhouses where they were spread to dry. Lavender cosmos blossoms bobbed in the unmowed highway shoulders.

51

Fifteen kilometers south of the city the little parade turned off the highway and rattled down a steep, unpaved track to the river side. Everyone climbed down from the truck and the statue of Vishwakarma was carefully handed down. Bhakta and four or five of the younger men stripped to their underwear and waded out into the river with the statue. They splashed some water on it and then set it free in the current. Shree Vishwakarma and his elephant immediately capsized and everybody laughed and cheered. Trailing a garland of marigolds the god floated downstream into some rapids, bobbing against rocks and through eddies, until he gradually disappeared from sight, on his long journey to the Brahmaputra and the Ganges and the ocean, which absorbs all. Bhakta and the other men cheered and splashed water on the spectators on the bank.

There was a sawmill nearby, and the crowd settled itself on a pile of scrap timber while the SOs poured beers and sodas and handed out the leftover snacks from yesterday's party. Man Bahadur was sitting off to the side of the group and noticed Suresh standing by himself. He put his hand on Suresh's shoulder and said, "Your brother Bhakta is trying to be back with us again."

"Yes," Suresh said, "He likes you all."

Man Bahadur hesitated a moment, then said in a low voice: "My god were we furious after he caused that fire. Coming home drunk and pushing around Chini Maya, then knocking over the kerosene lantern. Seven of the huts burned down. Not just his, but mine, Karchung's, Pradhan's. Did you know that? Our clothes, money, everything was burned. I was so mad I could have beaten the . . . but the poor bastard was so badly burned he passed out."

"He didn't mean to do it."

"Of course he didn't, but it happened."

"Did he pay compensation?"

"No, what could he pay? He lost everything too. The city corporation rebuilt the huts and the dasho gave us each a few thousand, but it didn't cover half of it. I had thousands saved for my daughter's dowry—all gone." Man Bahadur paused and watched the others eating and drinking and enjoying themselves. "But it was our karma I suppose. And he suffered for it more than any of us."

Suresh sat and said nothing.

"Do you want to know something?" Man Bahadur went on. "Even after what he did, I still like your brother, because he tries his level best to be a friend to all of us. With time he'll be back with us again. Not yet, but with time."

After the drinks and snacks were finished, no one wanted to leave, so they all sat on the grass and some of the men danced. They took turns dancing, clownishly, unselfconsciously, moving their legs, hands, and bodies in graceful, sinuous curves, as the rest sang and clapped. Bhakta took his turn dancing, in his cowboy boots and cap, with a happy smile on his burn-scarred face. The sawmill workers and a few farm women from nearby houses sidled over and clapped along shyly. Chini Maya, with Subhi on her back, stood with the women in her street sweeping crew, smoking a bidi, just watching and smiling with her shining black eyes and strong white teeth. Now and then the sun broke through the overcast and sparkled on the river, the paddies of ripening rice, and the circle of people.

The Shabrung, On Thangka and Videotape

Doctor Rani Chowdhouri felt elated when she finally signed her two-year contract with the United Nations Development Programme to serve as a pediatrician at the Bhutan Health Ministry's Samdrup Jongkhar District Hospital. It had taken several years—and several favors called in with acquaintances who had contacts in New Delhi—for her name to rise to the top of UNDP's roster. Contracts with the U.N. were plums: doctors earned two or three times what they could in all but the poshest clinics of Delhi or Bombay. And the professional challenge of working in a small hospital in the remote southeast border region of Bhutan would be invaluable for her career. Five months into the job she had done Pediatrics, Ob/Gyn, Internal Medicine—far more than she ever did at her husband's clinic near Calcutta, where she seldom treated cases more serious than ear infections and diarrhea.

But her elation was tempered with loneliness. She missed her husband and grown children so acutely that she was spending far more of her salary than she had planned on telephone calls to them. During her first months she had tried to befriend her Bhutanese colleagues, but despite their cheerful and polite relations at the hospital, lately she doubted that they would ever accept her as anything more than a visiting foreigner. Her bewilderment at the people's local customs compounded her isolation. Over and over again, just when she thought she had figured things out, she would make a gaff or be astonished by some completely unexpected behavior or event, and feel stupid. But weighing the pros and cons (which she found herself still doing almost daily), she decided that the money and the professional challenge were worth two years of isolation and loneliness.

On her first trip to her duty station, the idea of traveling by road and seeing the sights of Assam sounded adventurous, so she took a night train from Calcutta up to Siliguri and changed to a bus to the Bhutanese border. After thirty hours trapped in a long, slow-moving line of diesel-fuming trucks on the pothole-cratered highway, she decided that she would fly on subsequent home leaves. Not only was Samdrup Jongkhar remote in place, but it seemed remote in time as well. Of course, there were phones, and the few fax machines and photocopiers in government offices were relatively up-to-date. Nevertheless, some of the kinds of people that she saw wandering through town had not been seen in Calcutta (or at least in the nice suburbs, where she lived) in eighty or ninety years. On market days, peasants filled pack baskets with oranges, chilies and cheese from their farms, or ferns and mushrooms from the forest, and hauled them down from the hills on their backs to sell in the bazaar. Their wives brought in hand-loomed cloths of wild silk or nettle, or set up their looms in the shade and wove while their husbands haggled with Indian buyers. For fifty *paisa* or a rupee, old timers dressed in ragged red robes would spin their prayer wheels and say a prayer for you. Many were nearly blinded by cataracts, or had huge goiters, or had lost feet or hands to leprosy, but their afflictions never seemed to keep them from their posts in the sunshine at the entrance to the bazaar.

Some of the cases that came into the hospital were straight from the past, too. Cattle herders, both men and women, were brought in horribly mauled by tigers or bears. Accident victims whose wounds had been treated with folk remedies of herbs or dung were carried in weeks later with gross infections. She frequently treated children with eye and lung infections from living in smoke-filled huts, or with all kinds of parasites from lack of basic sanitation. The uneducated people's ignorance and apathy toward modern health practices irritated her, but at the same time, she found it intriguing. One particularly intriguing local practice was that many of these patients wore charms of one sort or another, which they swore protected them from sickness and harm. Many wore tiny leather pouches containing family relics around their necks, or knotted cords blessed by a lama, or little, plastic-laminated images of a Buddhist saint or Hindu god. Apparently they believed that the charms appeased the demons and spirits, or warded them off, or both. She had asked several of her Bhutanese hospital colleagues about them, but had never gotten a good explanation. She wished that she had time to learn to speak the hill folks' language so she could talk to them directly about the charms, but her job kept her too busy. Anyway, they made an amusing topic of conversation during her long telephone calls with her husband.

Rani was on-call one Sunday, and was just finishing her breakfast when the phone rang. It was Yeshe Dhondup, the health assistant on duty at the hospital's outpatient department. He explained that a man had just been brought up in a taxi from the truck depot with a severe wound on his arm. It was too much for himself and the nurse to handle alone. Rani made a little joke about leaving the phone off the hook, then said she would be right there. She gulped the rest of her coffee, threw her white doctor's jacket over her sari, and walked the ten minutes to the hospital. Already the puddles from yesterday's downpour were steaming in the sweltering sun, but the front of clouds building to the south promised another cooling monsoon soaking before long. As she entered the hospital lobby she glanced at the patients waiting outside the outpatient treatment room. Two dark complexioned, thin young women in cheap saris stood cradling crying babies on their shoulders. An unshaven man sat on the floor pressing a bloody rag to his foot. She recognized the man as one of the water sellers who made their livings filling empty cooking oil tins with water from the public tap next to her flat and wheeling them by the handcart load to sell to shanty dwellers in Darrang, the adjoining Indian town. The women were obviously Indians as well, taking advantage of the open border to get free medical treatment. There was an immigration and police checkpoint one kilometer north of town, but the actual border between Samdrup Jongkhar and the more populous, though unincorporated, Darrang was open, allowing workers, shoppers, and everyone else to flow back and forth freely. By habit she mentally diagnosed the cases as she walked past: the babies probably had ear infections—ampicillan and tylenol. No big deal. The water *wallah*—five or six stitches and a tetanus shot should fix him up.

In the OPD room a bare-foot peasant in a filthy *gho* lay on the examination table. A woman with Nepalese facial features dressed in a grubby tee-shirt and wrap skirt sat nearby in a chair. Yeshe Dhondup and the nurse (Rani could never remember her name) were trying to clean a suppurating wound on the man's forearm. Rani's eyes and nose immediately told her that gangrene had set in. The skin around the deep gash in his tricep had turned greenish and putrefied. His arm to the shoulder was badly inflamed.

57

The man had a glazed look in his eyes and was shocky definitely running a fever. She knew that the lower arm should be amputated. Yeshe greeted her with a smile and a polite bow as she walked over to the table.

"So, what is his story?" she asked.

"He is from a small village above Nganglam, *la*, about a day west of here," he replied in English. "His wife says that some bad men attacked him with a machete after he tried to stop them from stealing his cattle. The wife stopped the bleeding with leaves and herbs, but it got infected, *la*. It is paining him very much."

"No doubt. Um, ask her when it happened."

Yeshe translated, then told Rani, "She says six nights ago."

"Ugh. Poor man. Look, Yeshe, tell her that we will have to amputate the arm. We'll check him into the ward today and arrange the operation with the surgeon tomorrow morning."

Yeshe hesitated, seeming reluctant to translate to the couple.

"Go ahead, tell them."

Yeshe had not finished explaining when both the patient and the woman began jabbering angrily. The woman jumped to her feet and was pleading with him. With more energy than Rani thought he had in him, the patient forced himself up and was sliding off the table. "Quiet!" she shouted. The nurse ran to stop the patient, jabbering something, and got him to lie down.

"Yeshe, what's wrong?"

The wife was still pleading about something with Yeshe and he kept nodding and repeating something else in a reassuring tone of voice. After a moment the uproar subsided and the woman sat back down. Yeshe turned back to Rani. "He does not want to have his arm amputated, *la*."

"But he will probably die if we don't. You see the gangrene, don't you?"

"Yes, madam doctor, I told them that. But it does not matter. He says he would rather die."

"That's preposterous. Why?"

"They believe that when a person loses an arm or a leg, his reincarnation is born deformed, or missing that arm or leg."

"Oh, that's . . . " Rani almost said, "ridiculous," but then remembered that this was not her husband's suburban clinic at home and that she had made a resolution to herself to try to understand the ways of the people here.

Yeshe seemed to read her mind. "That is what these simple people believe in," he added with an apologetic note in his voice.

The determined looks on the patient's and his wife's faces told her that they would not budge and that there was no point in arguing. "All right, all right. All that we can do then is clean and dress the wound and give him a few weeks' supply of antibiotics and pain killers. Tell them that we will check him into the ward for rest and observation tonight. But we don't have room to keep him here longer than that. He probably won't make it, but you don't have to tell him that."

Yeshe translated and the couple assented; Rani tried to suppress her irritation at their foolishness.

After an orderly took the couple away and the three waiting patients were taken care of, Rani asked Yeshe if they should report the attack on the man to the police.

Yeshe shrugged. "There are many attacks like that these days. It happened at night; the patient did not get a good look at the men, so there is not much to report. But I will ask the administration officer to report it to the police anyway."

Rani had heard that outside of the main towns, the whole border region between Bhutan and Assam was unstable and dangerous. It was hard to know whether attacks

59

like this one were merely criminal or if they were politically-motivated. People said that they were either, or both. Several different groups either caused the instability or profited from it. Bodo insurgents periodically ambushed Indian police units or settlers who encroached on their tribal land. Ethnic Nepali Bhutanese agitators attacked remote villages and government facilities to retaliate for their expulsion by the Royal Government. Indian and Bhutanese security forces sometimes responded over-zealously to such attacks, and villagers feared them as much as the insurgents. Poachers took advantage of the disorder to feed the lucrative traffic in musk deer, rhino horn, and tiger parts for East Asian aphrodisiac suppliers. And run-of-the-mill robber gangs literally got away with murder. It was peasants like the patient who suffered most from it all.

As she was filling out the patients' treatment records, Rani asked, "Yeshe, the villager was wearing some sort of a charm around his neck, a plastic laminated photo of a lama with a long beard."

"Oh, yes la. That was a picture of the *Shabdrung*. During the commotion, I think you must have been hearing him beg the Shabdrung to protect him. Many villagers believe that he protects them. Especially now-a-days, with all the attacks and insecurity, the Shabdrung is very popular with them."

Rani smiled to herself as she finished signing the forms. Then she asked, "Uh, Yeshe, do you believe that charms, like the one the man had, can protect people?"

Yeshe hesitated. Rani tried to decide whether he would say what he himself believed or what he assumed she believed. "Yes, I do," he said after a moment. "Some are very powerful. You must be remembering the bad accident near Wamrong back in April, no? When the truck tried to get around the stopped bus and tipped over the cliff?"

"Yes, of course. It was horrible."

60

"Well, the one man who survived was carrying a picture of the Shabdrung in his wallet. He had some cuts and a broken wrist, but the other three men were killed."

Yeshe intrigued her. Here was a high-school educated, bright young man who attributed what to her was chance circumstance to the power of a charm. It wasn't so much this belief that intrigued her—after all, the majority of South Asia's uneducated people believed in this sort of thing, and, in more abstract ways, many of its more sophisticated, better-educated people did too. But few people ever seemed comfortable talking about beliefs like these. The thing that intrigued her was that Yeshe, unlike her other Bhutanese colleagues (and most of her Indian ones), was willing to talk about his personal folk beliefs like this one in a perfectly guileless and frank manner.

"Come to think about it," said Rani, "I have heard of the Shabdrung before. During my first month here I had to meet with some officials in Thimphu, and while I was there I bought a little painted cloth image for my husband at the government handicrafts emporium."

"Yes, a *thangka*."

"I guess. Anyway, the clerk said that the image was of the Shabdrung, at least I think that's what she said."

"Yes la, that's the first Shabdrung. Shabdrung Ngawang Namgyal. The Shabdrung in the photo around the patient's neck is the current reincarnation. The name 'Shabdrung' is sort of a title. It means, um, something like 'prostrate yourself at his feet.'"

One afternoon a few months later Rani was sitting in her office catching up on paperwork. It was late September, two weeks after the astrologers and lamas had forecast the end of the monsoon, but the rain still beat against her window. She gazed out at the road running downhill towards the bazaar. At a low point, a filthy, brown torrent

61

overflowed from the open drain and flooded garbage, sewage, and mud over the pavement. She was day-dreaming about some of the torrential downpours that she had seen as a girl in Calcutta when an excited voice at the door startled her.

"Madam doctor!"

She turned around and faced it. "Ah, Yeshe, please come in."

"I wanted to tell you. I just heard it from a nurse at the ward."

"My goodness, Yeshe," Rani laughed, "stop for a second and catch your breath. Whatever it is can't be that important."

"Madam Rani. You remember when you asked me about the Shabdrung?"

"You mean the lama on the gangrene patient's charm?"

"Yes. Well, they say that he is coming tomorrow!"

"What?"

"He will come tomorrow and do a *puja* to dedicate the new temple near the river."

Rani was confused. She wondered if she had misunderstood him. "I don't understand. The Shabdrung is real?"

"Of course."

She stared at him, amazed. "I, uh, just assumed that he was, uh, historical or something."

"No, la, He is real. He will come tomorrow."

"Well, then, where is he coming from?"

"From India. He lives in India somewhere. I don't know where."

Before Rani could ask more details, Yeshe jogged off to spread the word. This is bizarre, thought Rani, too bizarre to miss.

By evening, villagers had begun streaming into Samdrup Jongkhar. Out-of-towners roamed around the bazaar, and the cheap *thukpa* cafes and hole-in-the-wall bars were full of customers. Rani noticed their cooking fires and makeshift, plastic sheet shelters along the river as she walked back to her flat after work. She hoped for their sake that the rain would hold off, but from the sound of singing and laughing that drifted across the river, it appeared that they were not overly concerned about it. By eight o'clock the next morning, large crowds were milling about the bazaar and at the new temple grounds. Trucks and busses kept arriving from both sides of the border, packed with people, some from as far away as Tashigang District. When Rani made her way to the muddy field beside the new temple at midmorning, a group of townspeople and monks were just finishing setting up a shabby pavilion of canvas and plastic tarps. Fortunately it was a clear day, she thought, because the tent would surely collapse in the first downpour. She noticed Yeshe and some of the other hospital staff, who had brought their families and were already pouring thermoses of tea from large picnic hampers. They seemed pleased, if a bit surprised, to see her, and invited her to join them on their sheet of plastic. By eleven, Rani estimated that a few thousand people were packed onto the muddy field.

She never figured out how the word had gotten there, but all of a sudden the crowd began to buzz. Over and over she heard the name "Shabdrung" repeated by excited voices. Men ran and set fire to piles of juniper boughs at the entrance to the site; boys threw rocks to shoo away a pack of scrounging dogs. Thick, sweet juniper smoke began blowing over the crowd. People were coughing and wiping their eyes and laughing. Rani noticed for the first time that twenty or thirty blue-uniformed police officers, probably the whole Samdrup Jongkhar garrison, had taken up positions around the perimeter of the field. The young patrolman nearest to where she was sitting had a nervous look on his face, as if anticipating trouble. A senior officer, further down the field, held a video camera and seemed to be taping the faces in the crowd. Within minutes, the buzz crescendoed to a roar and the crowd was on its feet. Over the heads in front of her, Rani saw two Maruti jeeps and an open-bed light truck slowly drive down the gravel road towards the temple. By this time the crowd was cheering wildly and chanting "Shabdrung, Shabdrung" over and over. Rani found herself so caught up in the excitement that she cheered too.

To Rani, the actual appearance of the great Shabdrung and his entourage seemed to parody the people's wild enthusiasm for him. About a dozen youngish men, some in Bhutanese ghos, some in western style trousers and shirts, clambered out of the truck and ringed the pavilion. Seven or eight monks stepped out of the two jeeps. Even from where she sat, half-way back in the crowd, Rani could see that their red robes were shabby and mismatched. She got a brief view of the Shabdrung as the monks escorted him into the tent. He did indeed have the long black beard and the red, wedge-shaped miter of the image on her thangka, but he was short and overweight, and wore thick black plastic-rimmed glasses: the whole situation seemed comic to her. The crowd gradually hushed and sat down; the faces of the adults on either side of Rani beamed as brightly as their children's. Without any ceremony, the Shabdrung took a seat on the dais in the tent and the monks settled in rows on the ground flanking him. One monk began clanging a small pair of cymbals and the rest began chanting what Rani assumed were the dedication prayers for the new temple. After remaining reverently silent for five minutes or so, the crowd gradually began chatting among themselves. All the while the police officer with the video camera panned back and forth from the Shabdrung's people to the crowd.

Rani caught Yeshe's eye and sidled over to him. "Why are the police so interested in the Shabdrung?" she asked.

64

"The government does not like him," he whispered back.

"Why not?"

He looked over towards the officer with the video camera and ducked his head as the pan swept by. "I'll tell you later."

Rani shrugged, then turned her attention back to the tent. Craning to get a look inside, she noticed that the young men of the Shabdrung's cordon looked as edgy and nervous as the police. "If they don't like him, why did they let him into the country?" she whispered to Yeshe.

"They didn't. It was a surprise. And he would never get past the border checkpoint."

Maybe so, thought Rani, but there was no way that twenty or thirty unarmed cops could keep back—or disperse—a crowd like this.

After a half hour or so the Shabdrung stopped chanting and placed the cover back on his book of scripture. His monk attendants began distributing knotted wrist cords to the spectators in the front rows. The knots, she had once read, represented the endless knot of Buddhist *dharma*, an auspicious symbol of protection and integrity.

"Come on," said Yeshe as the crowd surged forward. "The cords have been blessed by the Shabdrung himself. Very auspicious, very powerful."

Rani joined the crush for the cords. She noticed that both the police and the Shabdrung's bodyguard were acting even more edgy than before. The press of smelly bodies behind her squeezed her against a frail-looking, elderly woman. She tried to apologize, but the woman only smiled gleefully at her with blackened teeth. A man further in front of her burst into sobs of joy as a monk handed him a cord. Fortunately, there are plenty of cords, she thought, or we would have a riot on our hands. As she received her cord, Yeshe reminded her that she should give a donation, so she dropped a twenty rupee note into the monk's sack. She

65

was amazed to see that the sack was full of grubby, worn five, ten, and even fifty rupee notes, all given by people whom, she knew from experience at the bazaar, typically haggled over paisa. When she made her way back to her original spot, she saw the Shabdrung's cordon leading him back to his jeep. Within five more minutes, the monks finished distributing the protective cords, climbed back into the jeeps, and the caravan slowly drove out through the crowd of bowed heads. Once they reached the paved road at the edge of the field, the drivers accelerated and were back across the border into India in no time.

The crowd gradually broke up. Rani joined Yeshe and his family in a large group that drifted back towards the bazaar. She felt happy to be part of the group, and to have shared in the community's event.

"So, you said that you would tell me about the Shabdrung, and why the government does not like him," she said to Yeshe.

"It is a long story, la."

"I would like to hear it."

Yeshe waggled his head. "O.K., I'll tell you. The Shabdrung was a lama prince from Tibet who came to Bhutan about four hundred years ago. He unified the country and brought peace and order. He built many *dzong* and defeated several invading Tibetan and Mongol armies. He wrote our laws and set up the first national government, with himself as the head of both religion and the state."

"Hold it." She laughed and touched his arm. "Wait. I mean the Shabdrung that dedicated the temple here today."

"Yes."

"But you are talking about the old Shabdrung, the one on the thangka, right?"

"He is the same. The man you saw today is the reincarnation of the first Shabdrung. Different body, but the same consciousness. The people believe that the man who

66

we saw today protects them and can bring peace and order just as the first one did."

By this time, they had reached the bazaar and the group began to split up. "Wait, Yeshe, before you go, this is all very interesting to me. Would you tell me one more thing? Why is the government against him?"

Before Yeshe could answer, he was interrupted by the noise of two canvas-topped Royal Bhutan Army trucks driving into the bazaar. Rani stopped and stared. One passed so closely that she could clearly see the army insignia—the Buddhist Wheel of the Dharma—painted on the fender. The trucks downshifted and jolted to a stop not far ahead. Fatigue-clad soldiers toting rifles clambered down from the backs and began fanning out. Seemingly by instinct, without any words said, the hundreds of people in the bazaar began bolting in all directions, behind shops, towards the residential areas, across the border, tugging their children along with them. Rani turned to Yeshe to ask what was going on but was startled to find that he and his family had disappeared. She felt her heart racing. She was alone and all the people around her were running for safety. A squad of soldiers jogged by her headed towards the site of the temple dedication. She edged against the wall of a shop and tried to be as inconspicuous as possible. At the Indian Oil fuel station fifty meters down the street, a pair of soldiers rounded up several ragged Indians at gun point and herded them towards the border. She heard angry voices up behind her and turned to look. At a public water tap, a soldier was forcing two water wallahs to pour out their full cans into the drain. The two then jogged past her, pushing their carts towards the border, swearing in Bengali, with the stern-faced soldier jogging behind them. Too late to catch the Shabdrung, she thought to herself as she watched them go by, so they take it out on the powerless ones.

67

She jumped and gasped at the sound of the harsh voice behind her. While watching the water sellers, she had not noticed the soldier approach from the other direction. She whirled around to face a short, tough-looking youngster in fatigues and a maroon beret gesturing menacingly at her with his rifle. She did not understand his words but knew exactly what he wanted.

"No, no," she stammered in English. "I'm supposed to be here. I work at the hospital." She glanced down at her sari and wished that she had worn her white doctor's jacket. She could hear the tone of panic in her voice.

The soldier repeated his order.

"Here, please," she pleaded and fumbled through her purse for her identification card. She finally found it and shook it in his face.

He lowered his rifle, took the ID card, and examined her photo, then her face, then the photo again. She wondered if he could even read, but felt relieved that at least he looked at it. After a few seconds he said "you waiting here" in bad Hindi and walked off with her card.

After a moment, her heart stopped racing and she considered slipping behind the shop and cutting through the back lots to her apartment. Then she remembered that the soldier had her ID card and that she would be in trouble without it. A few minutes passed, then five, when she saw two men approaching. They walked slowly, casually, talking with each other. One was a soldier, an older man with pronounced Mongoloid facial features, and was carrying a submachine gun clipped to his belt. Probably an officer, she decided. The other was a dignified-looking, middle-aged man with a neat mustache, dressed in a fashionable charcoal gray gho and stylish shoes. She had seen him around town but did not know who he was. Probably a government civil servant.

"Good afternoon," the officer said in English.

"Good afternoon," she answered.

"What is your good name, please?"

"Rani Chowdhouri. I work at the hospital here."

The officer took her ID card from his shirt pocket. "Mrs. Rani Chowdhouri..." he said, reading the card. "You are a doctor?"

"Yes sir, I work at the hospital here."

The government official cut in, "which agency do you work for?"

"Um, the Health Ministry...UNDP sponsors me."

"Ah, UNDP. I see." He took the card from the officer and looked her over for a few seconds. "I see that you have a protection cord on your wrist."

Rani glanced at the knotted cord that she had received from the Shabdrung's monks. She inhaled nervously but did not answer.

The official looked her straight in the eyes, then slowly handed her back her ID card. "Well, Mrs. Chowdhouri, you are free to go. But let me give you some good advice. Since you are a foreigner in our country, you may not know that the lama you saw this morning is a bad man. He is a...um...rabble rouser. In the future, you will be wise to avoid him and any people who support him."

"Yes sir, I understand."

"Good." Both men smiled faintly and nodded, then turned and walked back toward the troop trucks together.

Rani took a deep breath to settle her pounding heart, then walked quickly back towards her apartment. On the way, she yanked off the wrist cord and put it in her purse. At home, she sat alone on the balcony and smoked three cigarettes—more than she usually smoked in a whole week—and finally relaxed enough to think about doing her Saturday chores. After seven months of trying to get to know her Bhutanese colleagues and their society, she had never felt more bewildered and alone.

One day about a half year after the temple dedication incident, Rani gave Yeshe a lift back to Samdrup Jongkhar from a training workshop that he had attended in Tashigang. She herself was returning from a conference with the other U.N. medical workers in Thimphu, and, as she and the driver of the U.N. vehicle had long ago run out of topics of conversation, was delighted to have someone else to chat with for the last leg of the trip. Yeshe asked her about her family, and said that he had been surprised when she first told him about her married daughter and her son in the university, since he had assumed that she was only about thirty years old. Rani knew he was fibbing, but was pleased that finally she had reached the stage where at least one of her Bhutanese colleagues would tease her and flirt a bit.

She told him that, after the conference, she and some others had received permission to tour the dzong at Punakha, a few hours east of the capital.

"Ah, Punakha Dzong. It is very famous. Did you see the relic there?"

"Um, no. What relic?"

"The Shabdrung's relic of *Chenrezig*. It is very holy, very powerful."

"The Shabdrung whom we saw the police videotaping last year?" Rani interrupted. She meant it as a joke. As far as she knew, the incident had never been reported in the newspaper, and there had been no police repercussions, but she was not sure whether it was appropriate to joke about it.

Yeshe just waggled his head.

Guess I'll never know, thought Rani. "What kind of a relic is it?"

"It is a small statue of Chenrezig, the Buddha of Compassion. Long ago an important Tibetan lama died and was cremated and the statue formed miraculously from his vertebra bone. When the Shabdrung came to Bhutan, he

70

brought it with him. A Tibetan army invaded to try and get it back. They attacked Punakha Dzong, where the Shabdrung had hidden the relic. After some battles, the two armies made a truce and agreed that if the Shabdrung's soldiers brought the relic out and left it on the sand bar in the river, the Tibetans would take it and go back to Tibet. But then, instead of the relic, the Bhutanese army put an orange on the sand bar. The Tibetans thought it was the relic and took it and retreated."

"An orange?!"

"I am thinking perhaps they had never seen an orange before."

They both had a good laugh over that. "And the relic is still safe in Punakha Dzong?"

"Yes. That is why Bhutan has never been invaded by the Tibetans since. It is still protecting us today."

What a bizarre story, Rani thought to herself. "Well, Punakha Dzong certainly is a magnificent building."

"Yes, and very historic, too. It was the capital of Bhutan until the third king's time. All the kings were coronated there."

"Interesting. Well, then, let me ask you something. If the Shabdrung was the head of the government, how do the kings fit in?"

"Ehh. The kings come much later. You see, between incarnations of the Shabdrung, there were regents, who were more or less elected by the warlords of the different regions. But about one hundred years ago, the father of the first king defeated the other warlords. Then, with the support of the British, his son, Ugyen Wangchuck, formed the monarchy. And that ended the regent system."

"And the Shabdrung too, right?"

Yeshe waggled his head. "More or less."

When they finally reached the Samdrup Jongkhar border checkpoint late in the afternoon, Rani was surprised to recognize the immigration officer as the dignified-looking man who had confronted her during the temple dedication incident the previous autumn. He greeted her in a friendly tone, checked her documents and asked about her family and her work. As he handed her back her papers, he said, "I'm glad to see that you are no longer interested in that bad lama fellow."

Rani cheerfully replied that, on the contrary, she was still very interested in Bhutan's history and especially in the Shabdrung. In fact, her friend Yeshe Dhondup was just telling her about the Shabdrung's relic in Punakha Dzong, and how the monarchy had replaced the Shabdrung's original government system. She glanced at Yeshe, who returned a bland smile and impassive expression on his face. The official raised his eyebrows, but said nothing more. As they drove the last kilometer into town, Rani remarked that she was surprised that the official seemed to know so much about her.

"He is with the Home Ministry; it is his job to know," replied Yeshe.

By early April, hazy, white heat pulsing off the Assam plain enervated the town. Few village people came down from the hills to Samdrup Jongkhar's bazaar, busy full-time instead with their farm work, preferring the hill breezes to the humid swelter in town. There was a busy day when two forestry guards were brought in with gunshot wounds. Rani had assisted in the surgeries. Apparently they had surprised a group of men who were illegally felling teak trees in a forest reserve. The foresters tried to arrest them and got themselves shot in the process. It was never clear exactly who the assailants were: one of the guards told the police that he recognized them as ethnic Nepali Bhutanese who had disappeared after their village had been burned by the army during the unrest in 1991. The other guard believed that they were a gang of common thieves. Both guards recovered. Besides that, April and May were quiet. The monsoon broke in June, which put an end to dacoity for the season. In July, a mudslide knocked out the town's water supply intake, so the water wallahs reverted to filling their cans from the river. Rani was kept busy treating children with intestinal parasites for a month afterwards. She had not heard a word about the Shabdrung; the temple incident of the year before seemed like a bad dream.

On Saturday evenings, some of the hospital staff sometimes met at the Hotel Rabten, a "fooding and lodging" establishment in Samdrup Jongkhar's bazaar, for drinks and socializing. Even after more than a year and a half, Rani still felt lonely, so she always looked forward to a few cups of coffee at these get-togethers at the Rabten. On evenings when she was on-call, the nurse on duty knew to telephone the Rabten if she was not at her apartment. One Saturday evening in November she was surprised to see Yeshe appear there. As far as she knew, he typically spent every evening at home with his family. She was grateful to see him, since so far, none of the other staff members had shown up. In the harsh white light of the single fluorescent bulb, the bar's green-painted concrete walls had seemed unwelcoming and cold.

"*Kuzuzampo* Doctor Rani," he said loudly.

"Kuzuzampo Yeshe," Rani chuckled. It was obvious that he already had had more than a few drinks that evening. "Please," she motioned to an empty chair. "Join me." The chair legs grated loudly across the floor as he pulled it out and sat down at her table. The two men at the only other occupied table looked up and watched him. Rani recognized one as the Home Ministry man from the border checkpoint, but apparently Yeshe had not noticed him. "So, you aren't home with your family this evening?" she asked.

"No, la. Sonam went to her village for visiting her parents."

73

"I hope you're not supposed to be taking care of your children!"

"No, no. My children are gone. Sonam took them with her."

"Well, may I buy you a beer?"

Yeshe smirked and waggled his head.

"A small one, all right?" she teased.

Yeshe was in a happy and talkative mood. "You are reading *Kuensel*," he said, pointing to the thin newspaper folded on the table.

"Yes, I was reading it since no one else was here to talk with me. It is last week's issue."

Yeshe picked it up and glanced through the cartoon and the sports page quickly, then set it back down. The bartender brought a bottle of beer and a glass.

"Do you read the paper much?" Rani asked.

"Sometimes at my wife's shop I am reading it. She collects old ones for wrapping food only."

"The English or Dzongkha edition?"

He laughed. "For wrapping food there is no difference."

"Don't be naughty. I mean which language do you prefer to read?"

"Well, English is easier."

"How about your wife. Does she read English?"

Yeshe laughed. "No. She can't even speak it."

"How about Dzongkha, can she read that?"

"No. You see, our language is *Sarchopa* language, Tshangla. Niether of us knows Dzongkha very well."

Yeshe picked up the paper again and turned it to the front page. He smiled and pointed to the photo. "Ehh, here is the Shabdrung, the man you were so interested in." The photo was an old-style studio portrait of a young man in an elaborate oriental headdress and silk robes.

"I was reading that article," Rani said. It said that His Majesty and the queens presented a statue of the fellow in the photo, Shabdrung Jigme Dorji last week. Which Shabdrung was Shabdrung Jigme Dorji?

"The same!" said Yeshe brightly, with a smirk and a twinkle in his eye. Rani smiled and winked back at him, figuring that this obscureness had become his own little joke between them. "May I read it?" he asked.

"Of course."

Yeshe read through the article slowly, keeping his place with his finger and pronouncing the words with his lips. Rani drank her coffee and glanced around the room. She caught the immigration official glancing at them, then quickly turn back to his partner when he saw her smile and nod back at him. After three or four minutes Yeshe put the paper down.

"It is interesting story," he said.

"Yes, but for me it makes more questions than it answers. What is the background?"

"Why are you so interested in the Shabdrung?"

"I just am."

Yeshe gulped some beer from his glass. "O.K. Shabdrung Jigme Dorji was the last Shabdrung that was officially recognized by the government. He died in 1931. He was the uncle of His Majesty's father-in-law, the father of the *ashis*, the queens. You see, when His Majesty married the ashis in 1988, he married into the Shabdrung's family."

"Yes, that's what the article said. But his family is not the family of the Shabdrung we saw here in town last year, right?"

Yeshe snorted loudly and coughed. "Oh heavens, no. Different reincarnation, la."

"But he has the same consciousness as the one in the photo . . . and of the first Shabdrung."

"Yes," Yeshe said with a big smile. He chuckled and patted her hand. "You are understanding now, I think."

"Well, tell me this. If the previous Shabdrung died in 1931, why wait until 1995 to donate a statue of him?"

Yeshe, who was refilling his glass, put the beer bottle down next to him. A solemn look came over his face. He lowered his voice, although it still seemed loud in the nearly empty room. "There was trouble between Shabdrung Jigme Dorji and the second king, His Majesty's grandfather."

"So tell me," Rani said, arching her eyebrows and leaning across the table towards him. She was getting a kick out of Yeshe's conspiratorial manner and was enjoying playing along.

He took another drink. "O.K., here's the story, at least as I know. Shabdrung Jigme Dorji was recognized as the reincarnation of the Shabdrung sometime around the years 1905, 1910—about the time when the first king was coronated. Since the Shabdrung was still a boy, His Majesty the First King ruled the country by himself. Now when the second king was coronated, in the late 1920s, the two did not get along well. The Shabdrung was then a young man and maybe he was having too many parties, maybe he was giving too many favors to his family and his supporters. Anyway, at one point he gave grazing rights on Bhutanese land to some of his Tibetan relatives against the king's permission. When His Majesty blocked them, Shabdrung Jigme Dorji even sent a message to your Gandhi asking for India to support him. Then, one fine day, he was found dead." He paused, then whispered, "The official inquiry said that he killed himself, but there were rumors that he was strangled by His Majesty's men. And ever since then, the government has not recognized an official reincarnation."

"Juicy."

Yeshe nodded.

Rani bit her cheeks to hide her amusement at Yeshe's secretive manner. "But you didn't answer my question. Why the statue of him, after, what, sixty-five years?"

Yeshe shrugged. "I don't know. I guess for religious merit, like it said in the *Kuensel* article. Maybe also an offering from His Majesty's family to Shabdrung Jigme Dorji's family for, you know, condoling the old trouble."

"Huh. So that Shabdrung died in 1931. When was the present Shabdrung, the one we saw last year, born?"

"I am thinking that was in the late 1940s."

"It took fifteen years?"

"Oh, supposedly there was one other reincarnation before that, but he disappeared when he was a boy only. The present reincarnation was born near Tawang, which used to be in Tibet, but which is now in your Indian state of Arunachal Pradesh. The Indian army took him to India during their war with China in 1962, so that the communists could not capture him."

"Huh." Rani had not known of that incident of her country's difficult relations with Communist China. After a pause she said, "so, as far as the Royal Government is concerned, the institution of the Shabdrung ended in 1931 when Jigme Dorji died. But you and all those people who were at the temple dedication last year think that Bhutan still has both a king and a Shabdrung, right?"

Yeshe shifted in his chair. "His Majesty rules the country, and the Shabdrung protects it. The kings inherit from father to son; the Shabdrung is continuous."

"The Shabdrung's consciousness, anyway, right?"

He waggled his head. "And his relics. You are remembering the truck hijacking on the road from Geylegphug last month?"

"Yes."

"The two men who were not harmed had protective cords blessed by the Shabdrung. The man who was slashed with the machete did not." He paused for a moment, then pushed his chair away. "Excuse me."

Rani watched him walk unsteadily down the dark passageway behind the bar to the toilet. She checked her

77

watch. It was already ten o'clock and there had been no emergency calls from the hospital. It would be a quiet night. She went to the bar and paid for the drinks. When Yeshe came back from the toilet she watched the Home Ministry man beckon him over to his table. She could not hear what they said, but when Yeshe walked back to the table, she could tell he was upset.

"Is there anything wrong?" she asked.

"No, nothing wrong, la." His tone of voice had sobered. I am going only. Good night."

"What did he say to you?"

Yeshe looked at the ground and said softly, "Excuse me, I should not be talking so much with you. Good night."

One Friday morning a few weeks later a woman brought a ten month old girl with a chest infection into the outpatient clinic. Rani prescribed antibiotics and felt confident that the child would recover. She noticed, though, that the child had a deformed left arm, and immediately thought about polio. She asked the health assistant on duty, who happened to be Yeshe, to question the mother about this. He did, then answered tersely that the mother had assured him that the baby had been born with the deformity. Rani was disappointed not to get more information on the case: by the way the mother jabbered on, it was obvious that she told Yeshe more than that. These days, working with Yeshe was frustrating and bit saddening. Ever since he had been reprimanded at the Rabten, Yeshe, who had been so garrulous and helpful before, now gave her only the shortest possible answers to her questions. But later in the morning, after some prodding, Yeshe volunteered, "the baby was from the Nganglam area, where the fellow with the gangrene arm came from."

Rani thought for a moment, then remembered. "You mean the man we treated two summers ago, who did not want his arm amputated?"

"Yes, that same one. He died, you know. The mother says that the villagers think that her baby is his reincarnation."

"I'll be damned," whispered Rani to herself.

After lunch that day the hospital director sent Rani a note asking her to meet him in his office. After beating around the bush for a few minutes, he finally told her that the Health Ministry had terminated her contract, since she was no longer needed at the hospital.

Rani was stunned. "But I only have three months left on my contract . . . ," she sputtered. "And who will replace me?"

The director had a pained and embarrassed look on his face. He shrugged and said, "I'm sorry. That is what the ministry has ordered. The Immigration office told me that it expects you to leave Samdrup Jongkhar and return to India by Monday.

"You mean I'm being deported?" She could not believe it.

"Yes, it seems that way."

"But . . . why? I have done good work here, haven't I?"

The director shrugged. "Yes, you have. I don't know why."

Frantic telephone calls and faxes to the Indian embassy and U.N. office in Thimphu did no good. The U.N. program officer promised that he would investigate the termination before it was recorded in her personnel file, but he could not overrule a ministry decision. Since government offices were closed over the weekend, there was no way to appeal before Monday. He promised to send a driver and vehicle to Samdrup Jongkhar by Monday noontime to take her to the airport at Guahati, in Assam, so that she would not have to endure a long bus ride home to Calcutta. That weekend she packed up her apartment in a daze, selling what furniture she could to colleagues at the hospital and giving away the rest. None of her colleagues, least of all Yeshe, came by to sympathize with her, and she was too bewildered and bitter to seek them out. She wondered about how she could settle her phone bill on a weekend, then decided that the Telecommunications Department could stuff it. A messenger from the border control checkpoint came to her flat and told her to check with the immigration officer there before leaving. Monday came and she spent the day at her hospital office, fretting and dazed, waiting for the U.N. driver to show up and fearing that the police would come for her. The driver finally arrived late in the afternoon, but security curfews restricted driving through Assam after dark, so she spent the night in one of the rundown hotels in the bazaar. She drank several bitter cups of Nescafe to kill time on Tuesday morning while waiting for the immigration office to open at nine, which only increased the churning in her stomach. As she suspected, the officer on-duty was the well-dressed Home Ministry man.

With as few words spoken as possible, he confiscated her I.D. card and stamped the exit date on her passport, recording it in a ledger. When he finished he glanced at her hands, then up at her face. Finally, she thought, I'll get an explanation. He hesitated a second, as if unsure of whether to say what was on his mind.

"Well?" Rani asked, in a confrontational tone of voice.

"You aren't wearing your protective cord."

"What?" The question caught her completely off-guard. She did not understand what he was talking about.

"The wrist cord, that you got from the Shabdrung imposter. Where is it?"

The question seemed so bizarre that Rani involuntarily let out a snort of laughter, but, seeing the man's dead-serious expression, stifled it immediately. She had not even thought about the cord in well over a year, when she had

80

found it in her purse and thrown it away. "You . . . you want that, too?"

"Yes," he said firmly. "It should not leave the country."

"Well . . . I'm sorry. I don't have it anymore."

"What happened to it?"

"I threw it away. In a rubbish bin. Honestly, a long time ago."

The officer scanned her face for a moment, then frowned and wrote a note in his ledger. When he finished, he handed her back her passport. "All right then, Madam Doctor, you may go." He held out his hand, but she refused to shake it. He withdrew his hand. "I'm sincerely sorry if you have bad feelings. We gave you plenty of warnings, yet you have never seemed to understand. A small country like ours has room for only one ruler. We must protect ourselves."

A Certain Poetry to It All

The blare of the temple orchestra was so deafening, thought Nado, that if the deceased man's consciousness could not hear it, it must already have found a new incarnation. And somewhere far away, too—in Tibet, perhaps. He grinned to himself at the thought. After a moment the cacophony decrescendoed, and the monks sitting beside him glanced towards the prayer leader's dais for the cue to resume the chant. Nado sat in the back row of the monks who were performing the sixth and final day of a funeral *puja*. Each sat on a small prayer carpet on the polished wooden floor, his legs crossed under him. Two rows faced another two rows across the small temple. In the front rows sat the percussion and winds, with their cymbals, long handled floor drums, and silver oboes; in the back sat the chorus. Along the south wall, flanking the dais, sat the tuba players, each resting the silver filigreed bell of his huge brass horn on the floor between a row of maroon-robed monks.

The other chanters read aloud from unbound stacks of scripture, laid out neatly on the floor in front of them.

Nado did not need a book; he knew by heart this funeral ritual and, indeed, most other rituals in the doctrine of the Kagyupa order of *Mahayana* Buddhism. He was as qualified as the chant leader to lead the ceremony, but was only twenty-nine years old, and the honor of leading should go to an older man. Besides, he liked sitting in the back row with the younger monks, where he could discretely preoccupy himself with his own thoughts. His eyes freed from the printed pages, he lifted them as he chanted, and let them wander over the gently swaying heads of close-cropped black hair, and around the familiar temple.

He gazed at the faded, smoke-darkened murals on the west wall. Near the open door were the familiar images of *Guru Rimpoche*, of *Chenrezig*, and of Shabdrung Ngawang Namgyal. Around the border of one mural were small portraits of the various lamas who had overseen this monastery, all in the same stylized, seated lotus pose, floating on a cloud or a lotus blossom, like the images of Lord Buddha himself. What were the names of those old lamas? When had they lived? He did not know. The images were so faded that you could barely make them out. Another mural depicted a story from the life of Milarepa, in which the great Tibetan poet-saint saved a deer from a hunter. The saint was sitting at his meditation cave, shielding the deer and converting the man to Buddhism, admonishing him never to kill any sentient being. Actually, Nado really could not see this particular mural from where he sat, blocked by one of the intricately carved and brightly painted roof pillars, but he had always liked the story and knew the mural well. The metaphor pleased him: Milerepa, the poet, protecting a deer, and offering peace of mind to all.

In the center of the north wall was the temple's main altar, with the auspicious symbols of the *dharma*—the endless knot, the wheel, the lotus, the victory banner, and the rest—carved into its sides and brightly painted in red and blue, yellow and green. On the lower level of the altar were clusters of lit incense sticks, each with a faint, thin plume of aromatic cedar smoke curling upward; and a rack of forty-nine vegetable shortening lamps (butter was too expensive to burn in the lamps these days), with forty-nine tiny flames cheerfully flickering and bobbing in the draft. On the altar's upper level stood a large bowl with a pineapple surrounded by bananas and cucumber spikes, all carefully arranged. Scattered around was a disorderly arrangement of small statues of the buddhas, *torma* flowers sculpted from butter, a pitcher of holy water, a peacock feather, and a dish of cash offerings. Two old, varnished elephant tusks flanked the altar's sides.

A side altar had been set up for the deceased. The little altar, like the prayers they were chanting, was intended to guide the dead man's consciousness through the *bardo*, the threshold period between its departure from the dead body and entrance into a new womb. The deceased had been the father of one of the monks at this monastery, and one of its wealthier benefactors. The corpse had been cremated a few days after its death, as was the custom to prevent ghosts from inhabiting it; but now, a week later, prayers were still needed to guide the consciousness on its search of a high reincarnation. Just as in life a person needed guidance in recognizing the illusory nature of this world, so the consciousness needed help in avoiding the temptations and illusions of the bardo. Of course, the puja helped relieve the family's grief as well. The side altar was decorated with a drawing of the man (his shadow, they called it), and brightly colored tormas, and various goodies—a box of cookies, a bottle of Thums-Up cola, a bottle of Dragon Rum—to help the consciousness along its way. The monks liked doing these funeral pujas because the deceased's family provided lavish and delicious meals throughout the entire six days, and gave them gifts of cloth and cash.

The monks chanted the prayers in low, nasal tones, a weird, reverberating sound that took much practice to master. The dialogue of tones and words flowing back and forth between the two facing rows mesmerized a listener and effected him weirdly; drawing him in and then pushing him back out, as if rolled in the surf at the ocean shore. The chant leader set the tempo with small, clanging cymbals, speeding up or slowing down at the appropriate points in the prayer. The drummers picked up the rhythm on their temple drums, finely carved and painted with grinning skulls, which they held upright on the floor on long handles and beat with curved sticks. The chanters finished each verse with a sustained, low, decrescendo tone, then rested as the cymbals, oboes, and long deep horns blared their primordial clanging, jangling, and booming. After a minute or two, the orchestra would taper off and the chanting would resume.

During the next rest in the chanting, while the orchestra blared, Nado gazed out the low window on the south wall behind the dais. From his place in the back row he could see Talakha Mountain, twenty kilometers south across the Thimphu Valley. Its forested slopes and pointed rock peak dwarfed the capital city's massive fortress *dzong*, its apartment blocks and radio towers, and the puny villages and rice paddies scattered along the valley floor. He thought of the deceased's consciousness, and the guidance their prayers were offering it, and smiled wistfully to himself. The dead man's consciousness was lucky in a way, for no such clear cut directions were ever available for the living. Nado knew no prayers or rituals that could provide specific answers to the indecision which sometimes nagged him. He squinted his eyes, so that all he could see was the afternoon's sun rays streaming through the window and glowing on the chant master's shoulders, on the cymbals, and the polished amber pine floor planks. And yet, he thought, directions or no directions, it was the beauty of

85

small, mountain temples like this and the poetry of these rituals that made him choose this career, and which kept him here.

One day a month or so later Nado was told that Kencho, his old friend from the monastic school, had telephoned to say that he would be coming up to Dorjedra for a visit. The telephone line had only a few weeks ago been strung up from Thimphu and phone calls were still a novelty among the Dorjedra monks. Nado figured that, like the electricity, which had caused such a sensation when the power lines were installed two years ago, the novelty of phone calls would soon wear off. Soon they would depend on the phone just like the electric lights. Nado was always glad to see Kencho, an energetic man with modern and refreshing ideas. They had been the top students of their batch at the monastic school, which is what originally brought them together, and visits to each other's home villages over the years had strengthened the friendship.

Kencho had taken an unorthodox route after he finished school. He never formally joined the monk body, but instead moved in with an ambitious relative in Thimphu, a civil service official who was rapidly climbing the promotion ladder. Like Nado, Kencho spoke English fluently. He also had an easy confidence about meeting government big shots, foreign expatriate development workers, and other people in prestigious positions. The last that Nado heard was that Kencho was running a successful "business," if it could be called that, performing pujas and other Buddhist rituals for these influential—and rich—people.

Kencho hiked up to Dorjedra on Saturday, a day off when Nado did not have to teach the novices. Nado met him outside the long barracks-like building where many of the monks had their rooms.

"Kuzuzampo la. How long did it take you to walk up?" Nado asked.

86

"Good morning. Oh, an hour or so, not bad." It was a sunny morning in July; the monsoon's afternoon rain clouds had not yet piled up, and sweat dripped from Kencho's forehead. "I saw some of your students heading down the trail," he said.

"Off to hang out in the bazaar, then watch the football match this afternoon. They love Saturdays."

"Have you been to a match yet this summer?" Kencho asked.

"I caught the one two weeks ago, when I had to go into town. A lousy game, but it was fun to watch."

"Good. I'm glad you're getting out of here now and then." Nado led Kencho to his room. At the door, as customary, they removed their shoes.

"Here Nado, I brought a treat from Thimphu," Kencho said, and pulled a plastic sack from his monk's red shoulder bag.

Nado laughed softly and shook his head at the chocolate eclairs in the sack, then took them into his little kitchen room. He returned with a thermos flask of butter tea and a small round basket of *zow*. He put the eclairs in the serving basket with the zow.

"I actually like your room," Kencho said as he settled himself cross legged on a prayer rug on the floor. "It's neat, cosy. You've got a little cooking room too."

"Haven't you seen my room before?" asked Nado.

"No, I haven't been up here since the new quarters were built and the electricity brought in. When was that? A couple of years anyway."

"Yes, two years, a little more really."

Kencho gazed around at the room and the furnishings: the small cooking room off the entrance, the main room, just large enough for a bed, clothes chest, and book case, a little window overlooking the valley, Nado's simple personal altar, the photos and calendars that decorated the

87

walls. "Very nice. Compact, tidy, clean. Not as depressing as I thought it would be."

"Depressing?"

"Well, you know, musty, smoky, dark—monkish. No offense, la, but some of the old quarters up here were rather appalling. Anyway, . . . is it warm in winter?"

"In the day the sun warms it up pretty well. Of course we don't have stoves for heat at night, so it's cold then. These rooms are well-built though, so no drafts."

They sipped tea and tried the eclairs, then settled into munching the zow kernals, which even Kencho admitted he preferred. Kencho pointed to one of the pictures on the wall. "Where did you get that," he laughed. On the wall among the company of the King of Bhutan, the *Je Khenpo* (Bhutan's chief abbot), Dilgo Kyentshe Rimpoche (an important Bhutanese lama), and Tibet's Dalai Lama was the American star Tina Turner. Nado laughed. "My brother gave it to me. I think he got it in India. I like it."

"Have you ever listened to her tapes?" Kencho asked, smirking.

"No, I don't think so."

"Someday I'll find one for you."

Nado nodded and smiled.

They drank another cup of tea and talked about friends and family, their conversation switching between their native Tshangla and English language as suited them. After a while Nado asked, "I hear that you are doing pujas and prayers and that sort of thing on your own in Thimphu."

"Yes."

"Does it keep you busy?"

"Busy enough. I do a ceremony or two each week. I did a sickness puja for a department director's young daughter the other night. This afternoon we'll bless the house of the new director of the United Nations office. For most of the foreigners in Thimphu, it's probably really just a house warming party, but they like to have the prayers, the prayer flags out front, and all the rest of it."

"You do a lot of ceremonies for the foreigners."

"Yeah, more and more. They like it. And I guess they like being able to talk with a monk who speaks English. They tell their friends, word gets around." He paused and smiled. "You know, they call me 'Lama Kencho.'"

Nado nodded, but did not return the smile. "I'd heard. Do you tell them you're a lama?"

Kencho noticed Nado's cooler tone. "No, of course not. That's just what they call me, la. I . . . I'm not sure some of them even know the difference between a regular *gelong* and a lama. And since only a handful of senior monks and real lamas speak any English, the foreigners never have a chance to get to know them."

Nado had not really meant to put his friend on the defensive, so smiled and said, "You must make good money, no?"

"Not so much, but enough. Most Bhutanese officials are generous because it gains them religious merit and prestige among their guests. The foreigners are too. For prestige, I suppose, or maybe it's just their way. Most of them are pretty rich. But besides the money, I like meeting these people. They are interesting, they've traveled around and seen things, no? Their world is bigger and more interesting than the world of most monks."

"Yes, I'm sure it is."

Kencho glanced at his watch. They had been talking for two hours and he had not yet mentioned what he had come to discuss. "Nado, before I have to get going, I wanted to ask you something. I heard that you've been offered a position on the administration staff with the Central Monastic Body."

"Yes. Word gets around, doesn't it?"

"What would you do?"

89

"Um, curriculum development; training and supervising the instructors at the monastic schools."

"Training?"

"You see, the Health and Education Ministry, UNICEF, some other agencies want to see the monastic schools include English, hygiene, math, basic health care, that sort of thing in the training for young monks. Let them then go back to their villages and teach the farmers. His Majesty has been pushing it, and the Monastic Body is finally seeing that it might be a good idea."

"Well?" asked Kencho.

"Well what?"

"Will you take the position?"

Nado gazed out the little window of his room at the view of the forested mountain slopes and smiled to himself. "Um, I haven't decided yet," he answered after a moment.

"You haven't decided la? I'm surprised that you even want to think about it. It sounds like an important position. I'd take it in a flash."

Nado sighed. "Oh, yes, I guess it's important. Training the young monks to be more socially relevant and productive. I suppose your civil service and foreigner friends think that most of us monks are pretty backward, don't they?"

"Well, Nado, they have a point, don't they? Excuse me please, but just look at most of the boys you teach. They don't know more than a few words of English. They are down at the hospital being treated for diarrhea every other month because they don't bother using a latrine or washing their hands. When they go back to their villages, they're just as backward as the uneducated farmers."

"But they do know how to say the prayers and do the ceremonies that the villagers want, don't they?" Nado said.

Kencho grinned. "Of course. And I'm not saying that isn't important la. But don't you think that they could be doing a lot more to help their villages?"

"Yes . . . " Nado said. He was gazing at his small meditation altar and forgot the next thing that he wanted to say. He was thinking about his own village in Mongar; how the few monks at the village temple were as uneducated and superstitious as the rest of the old farmers; and how the children who went to school felt frustrated with the backward lifestyle and wanted to move to the towns to work. He knew that the Monk Body had honored him by offering the position; it had made him proud to think that they valued him this much. Yet that was part of the problem.

Kencho saw him thinking and waited a while before adding, "I came up here to encourage you to take the position. You're the perfect one for it, Nado. You, me . . . there are only a few monks our age in the whole country that really understand the modern world. And you're such a good teacher. The boys love you."

"Thanks."

"It's your ticket up, you know. You could be a senior administrator by the time you're forty, la. Maybe have one of the monk body's seats in the National Assembly. Would you rather stay here and teach the novices for your whole life?"

"I like it here, teaching the boys. Besides, in Thimphu I'd be in some small, dark office dealing with other officials all the time."

"But . . . "

Nado held up his hand to interrupt. He remembered the other thing he had wanted to say. "But that's not the real reason that I haven't made up my mind about it. You're right, la. The village monks need to do more for the farmers than only prayers and pujas. And it is a chance for advancement for me. But the main reason I can't decide is that I'm also thinking about moving to Dharamsala for a few years. I want to study meditation under a Tibetan lama there." A look of surprise flashed on Kencho's face. Nado felt faintly embarrassed and hurried to justify himself. "I suppose your friends in the government, and your foreigner friends, and even some in the Monastic Body will think that is selfish and, um, foolish. But it's something that I've been thinking about for a long time, and if I take the new job . . . you know how one thing leads to another . . . I'll probably never get another chance to go."

Kencho was looking at the floor. "I didn't know you were thinking of that."

"No, I haven't told anybody."

Kencho nodded and gazed around the room. After a moment stood up. "Yeah, well Nado. You know we're friends and I want you to do well. If it were me, I'd take the job. I just wanted to give you, you know, my advice about it."

"Thanks Kencho. Are you going now?"

"Yes, I have to do the house blessing puja at two o'clock."

"At two? You'll be late, won't you? It will take that long just to walk back to town. And it's starting to rain."

Kencho stepped out the door, put on his sneakers, and took his umbrella from his bag. The afternoon summer monsoon clouds had piled up and a light, warm rain had begun to spatter the dirt on the trail. "No problem. A half hour down the trail and then it's only a ten minute drive into town."

"You have a car?!"

"No, a motorbike," he laughed. "Don't look so surprised for heavens sake. I parked it at the trailhead. Goodbye now. Let me know what you decide. Give me a call or visit when you come to town."

Nado clasped his friend's hand. "OK."

Kencho opened his umbrella and set off down the trail back toward the valley.

"Thanks for coming up today," Nado called out.

Kencho waved and was soon out of sight.

Summer went along pleasantly up at the monastery while Nado put off deciding about the job offer. What to do, la? He did not know. He liked the routine of his life: it encouraged procrastination. He awoke at five o'clock each morning to pray and meditate, a time when the air was still and clear; when he could watch the sun rise over the ridges and steam the dew off Dorjedra's rooftops, while dawn shadows still cloaked the city below. After breakfast of tea and rice, while the air was still cool, he often took exercise by hiking a half hour to the base of a cliff, where in the 13th Century the monastery's founder had meditated. The lama's body had left an imprint in the rock in the shape of a *dorje*, from which a clear spring now flowed. Later each morning he taught the novices to read scripture and chant prayers. The boys made memorization into kind of a game, in which they chanted the words back and forth to each other. They learned pretty well this way, although Nado knew that for many of them, only the sequence of words mattered, that they would never really grasp the words' meaning.

There was always a big meal at midday: tea, a huge vat of rice, and curries of hot chilies, potatoes, ferns, meat, or whatever else they could get. A few old men and women, who had retired from farming and raising families in the valleys to live their last years at Dorjedra in religious retreat, supervised the domestic chores. The novices took turns helping them, gathering firewood, fetching water, and the like. Monks, novices, and retreat people ate together, sitting in rows on the flag stone terrace outside the cook house, each day with a full rice basket and curry bowl and tea cup. On weekends, some boys were sent to the bazaar for the week's food, purchased with donations or given free by pious stall keepers. Once every few months three or four were sent down with an empty cooking gas cylinder. It was hard work carrying the heavy steel bottle down the trail, hitching a ride to the fuel station, and lugging the even heavier full one back up. But for the boys, it was a holiday from prayers and a chance to hang out in the city for a few hours and buy candy. And with three pairs of arms, the cylinder was not really *that* heavy to carry.

Most afternoons, after his nap, Nado spent by himself reading scripture or practicing meditations. He would watch the monsoon clouds build over Talakha Peak, then the rain curtain sweep up the valley, until it finally drummed on his corrugated steel roof. The novices were supposed to study too, or at least do housekeeping chores, but more often than not they would end up playing with Dorjedra's pack of dogs, or winging stones at the troop of langurs which fed in the trees on the slopes below. Nado sometimes reminded them of the story of Milarepa, the hunter, and the deer, to which they all piped up "we should never kill animals." They would feel terrible if their stones ever actually hit a langur. But since the beasts always fed just out of their range, and leapt to the next bough if a stone ever came close, the boys figured that technically there was little risk of disobeying the teaching.

Some of the dogs that lived at the monastery also loved to torment the langurs. When the troop appeared in the trees, they would tear down the slope, barking insanely, and the langurs would scatter, leaping into treetops further down the mountain side. The dogs then trotted back up to the boys with self-satisfied looks. But others of the dogs were such old wrecks, so mange ridden, that they spent their days collapsed in the shade, scratching their bald pink hides raw. Nado sometimes thought that it might be more compassionate to end these dogs' misery and kill them. Compassion to animals was important: who knew whether one of the wretched curs might have been a relative in a previous life? But to kill them, he knew, would result in

94

negative karmic consequences, whether in this life or another, so whether compassionate or not, it was best to stick by the Buddhist teachings. After all, perhaps previous incarnations of Dorjedra's dogs had ignored the dharma and killed and sinned, and the present ones were now suffering the consequence.

Nado liked teaching the boys because they made him laugh. Sometimes they reminded him of his own childhood. He was from a small village in the Mongar District, where generations of farmers had terraced whole mountainsides of jungle into steps of tiny corn fields and rice paddies. He was the third boy in a family of eight. One brother and sister also led religious lives, another brother worked in the southern border town of Geylegphug. The others were farmers. He had gone to the primary school in the nearest large village and after passing Class 4 at the top of his class, went to Mongar Junior High School and from there, to one of the prestigious high schools in Thimphu. There were enough brothers and sisters at home to tend the family's farm and cattle, so his parents did not mind him being away. They were proud of him, really, and boarding at the schools, he was one less mouth that they had to feed.

It was in high school in Thimphu that the kids gave him the nickname Nado—"Blackie"—for his dark complexion. Dorji Gyeltsin was the name that the lama had given him as a baby, but he liked his new nickname and it stuck. He was one of the best students in his class, taking second in the science examination and scoring high in English. Most of the other students at the prestigious school—the children of government officials and wealthy, influential families—went on to university in India or began cushy, secure careers with the royal government. Nado could have followed these routes too, and done well, but his heart was not in it. What he really wanted to do was to become a monk and study Buddhist dharma. While most of his classmates were cramming for the university or civil service entrance exams, he was entering a monastic school with uneducated village boys ten years younger than himself. During the first year he suffered bouts of doubt and depression when he thought he had made a foolish choice. But as he began to learn the prayers and scriptures and think critically about their meaning, and to appreciate the beauty and poetry of the rituals, he became confident that his decision had been the right one. He had a discipline for learning from his years in the government schools, and mastered the monastic curriculum in only three years. But his success drew on more than just disciplined study habits. In the government schools he studied because it was expected of him. In the monastic school, for the first time, he learned because the material spoke to his heart.

Sometimes even these days he still doubted whether he had made the right decision to enter religious life and reject so much of the modern world. It was particularly frustrating that the other adult monks at Dorjedra seemed uninterested in taking a practical, scientific approach to the day-to-day operation of the monastery. It was not merely that none of the others ever explained things like the connection between bad sanitation and disease to the boys. It was the prevalent attitude of doing as little as possible to improve the monastery buildings or to make their lives easier, healthier, and safer. Rain leaking through a neglected roof gradually destroyed priceless old murals. Silver fish bugs slowly ate their way through their library of irreplaceable scriptures. The new electrical system had been out of order for two weeks, probably from something as simple as a line crossed or down somewhere, but no one had bothered to investigate and to arrange for its repair. Even the uneducated farmers in his family's village could evaluate problems like these and work out solutions to most of them. Many of the monks though just did not seem to care, content to say the prayers that were expected of them and eat their daily meals.

Of course he agreed with Kencho that some instruction in health care and other useful subjects was needed for novice monks. But as to whether he was the person to develop the new monastic school curriculum, he still could not decide. It was not merely that he preferred a simple monastic life to one of schedules and meetings and phones in a Thimphu office; or even his desire for doing advanced study in Dharamsala. There was another factor, which he had not mentioned to Kencho because it conflicted with the very thing that motivated his friend's life. Nado understood full well that his new job offer was an honor and a ticket to promotions and prestige. But it was just this desire for advancement that held him back. It was human nature to desire prestige, wealth, influence—but his study of Buddhism taught him that these were illusions of the material world. Desires like these trapped a person into the material world's endless cycles of suffering. To be detached from desire was the way to become an enlightened person.

It was a tricky balance, a dilemma that he thought about often. Was the older monks' reluctance to improve their living standard the detachment from desire that Lord Buddha taught, or simply apathy? Was it selfish laziness to take no effective actions to try to alleviate the poverty and ignorance of most of the people in the country, or the dysentery and respiratory infections that plagued the children? Or was their inaction grounded in a sage acceptance of their Buddhist beliefs: that in this world, people suffered, and it was their karma to do so? He knew that clever people could argue a reasonable-sounding justification for just about anything. Was his attempt to detach himself from the desire for prestige a step toward enlightenment, or was it a justification of his own inertia to change his comfortable lifestyle? He loved the beauty of the temple and the Buddhist teachings; but did he love them for their intrinsic value or only because they were better than the prosaic life of offices and shops and cars and diesel fumes in the city? These thoughts washed back and forth in his mind that summer, like the sounds of the prayers flowing back and forth between the rows of chanters in the temple. The funeral prayers gave clear directions to the dead, but for his choice, religion seemed to offer no definite guidance.

That September Nado met with his superiors in the monk body and told them that he would not take the position. They reluctantly approved his request for a three year leave to study meditation under the famous lama in India.

The thing that he remembered most vividly about the little hospital in the Gidakom Valley was how hard the wind blew during the afternoon. As if turned on by a timer, at about one o'clock the gusts began whistling through the eaves, rising and falling, sometimes as deafeningly as the horn blasts during the intervals of a puja. If he listened to the sound, it irritated him and distracted him, so that his only thought was wishing it would stop. At such times he tried instead to focus his attention on the willow and poplar trees along the river below the hospital, which thrashed and bowed in the wind. Some days, before he knew it, the hospital staff would be ringing the supper bell and the trees would be standing still in the calm, early evening shadows.

Nado had plenty of time that winter and spring to think. After he finally made his decision to go to India, and his leave was approved, he had spent a month visiting with his family in Mongar and brother in Geylegphug. When he returned to Dorjedra, he felt weak and run-down. Every morning he woke up with a mild fever, which would just not go away. He kept postponing his departure, not having the energy to face it, and hoping that a few weeks of rest would make him feel better. He sent some boys to the traditional hospital in town for herbal medicines, vile tasting powders that are drunk as hot teas three times a day, to restore his energy and strength. He knew that sickness, as understood by the medicine system of Mahayana Buddhists, was due to imbalance of the body's wind, phlegm, and other humours. Not only proper medicines, but also correcting the emotional causes of the imbalance were necessary to get well. He stopped teaching and spent days meditating on the causes of the imbalance, trying to free himself from them to restore his health. But of all the countless thoughts and actions of his life, let alone the unknowable ones of previous lives, it seemed impossible to identify a single cause. The fever hung on, and he developed a dry cough. He became frustrated at his poor health and began to fear that something was seriously wrong. He found himself vaguely desiring to turn the calendar back to a time when he was healthy, and envying the health and energy of the young novices as they scampered down the trail to town on Saturdays. The longer he postponed his departure, the more bitter with himself he had gotten. The more that bitterness and fear and envy clouded his thoughts, the sicker he had become.

He also had plenty of time that winter and spring to get to know the other patients at the hospital. On sunny afternoons the staff set up a *karom* board on the porch, and patients and their families spent hours playing and watching this skittle board game. Most were old lepers who had lost fingers and feet, or patients with more advanced stages of tuberculosis than his. They were simple farmers from remote villages who had been too ignorant to seek medical treatment at the government clinics, or had relied solely on pujas and folk remedies until they now were too far wasted to recover. But despite their bleak prognoses, most of them remained merry day in and day out. They chatted and played dice and karom with their new-found hospital friends. If a patient's relatives came to visit, sleeping on floor mats in the ward for days or weeks at a time, the other patients made friends with them too. Each day

99

they stuffed themselves with rice and curry—delighted to eat free meals at the government's expense—and fed scraps to the dogs which slunk up from a nearby village. One old leper even managed to knit a sweater holding her knitting needles between her thumbs and finger stumps. There were a few sad days in the winter when one TB patient died, but the old timers did not seem to let it depress them, and their cheerfulness lifted everyone's spirits.

It had not been until the previous November, two months after he had returned from visiting his family, that Nado finally realized what was wrong with him. He received a letter from a sister telling him that his brother in Geylegphug had been diagnosed with tuberculosis. Nado at once suspected that he also had caught the infection and decided to get it checked out. The hike down to the road was an exhausting ordeal, but luckily he quickly caught a ride to Thimphu's "western" hospital. The doctor ordered tests, and Nado had spent a day standing in a crowd of jostling patients and crying children and formaldehyde and urine smell at the pathology lab. When the test result turned out positive, he spent another day in line for a chest x-ray. The doctor said he had TB, but that it was in an early stage, and a six month course of antibiotics and quarantine at the Gidakom sanitarium would probably cure him.

Now, for the first time since he had gotten sick, he understood the physical cause. A bacterial infection, nothing more; something that he had studied in high school biology class. Even if he did not understand the karmic cause that ultimately underlay it, he could take the antibiotics that the doctor prescribed, and focus on regaining peace of mind. With understanding his fear lessened, and with it the bitterness and envy. From that day his anxiety melted away and his health gradually returned. On warm afternoons at the hospital, as he watched the old lepers play karom and feed the scrounging dogs, he wondered if they understood the connections between mind and health, or if they were just naturally cheerful. The effect was the same, regardless, he concluded. Throughout March and April he watched the willows along the river thrash and bow in the afternoon wind, yet every day, barely perceptibly, grow greener and fuller with swelling buds. In early May, he was discharged.

Siliguri, in the thin strip of West Bengal between Bihar and Assam, is at its hottest and stickiest in May, before the monsoon breaks. A Tata bus idled at a railroad crossing on the outskirts of this industrial city, waiting for a train to pass. Diesel fumes wafted into the windows on a breeze. Diesel smelling or not, the breeze brought relief from the suffocating smell of the sweating passengers. All the seats were crammed full with riders, and standing passengers packed the aisle. Shrill Hindi movie music blared from the speakers that the bus driver had rigged up above his seat. The rowdy young men sitting up on the luggage rack stamped their feet on the roof to the beat. The racket made Nado think of the blaring noise of a funeral puja. He laughed to himself at the irony. He felt light-hearted and free. He was out of the hospital and on his way across India, with no responsibilities or cares. He noticed that the bus conductor, a rather bullying young man, was arguing with a Bhutanese man who was sitting further up the aisle, demanding that he pay an additional fare for the leg of the trip between Jalpaiguri and Siliguri. He insisted that the ticket the Bhutanese fellow had bought in Jaigoan was only good for the first leg, up to Jalpaiguri. From there to Siliguri cost 15 more rupees. I hope he doesn't fall for it, Nado thought; the Indians must take us Bhutanese for complete hicks.

Nado thought back about the odd experience he had that morning while waiting for the bus at Jaigoan, just across the border from the Bhutanese town of Phuntsholing. He had been sitting under a shady pipul tree, watching a skinny and ragged boy tugging on the sleeves of

101

passersby on the crowded street, begging for *paisa*. A fruit stall vendor was talking to a police officer further up the street, all worked up about something, pointing repeatedly at the boy. Nado watched the officer walk quickly towards the boy, and then the boy bolt when he noticed him approaching. The boy glanced around in panic as he ran, looking for a way to escape. As the cop closed on him, he caught Nado's eye. His big, scared eyes, shining black, reminded Nado of a deer's. The boy ran behind Nado and clung to his maroon robes and blurted in Hindi "protect me, guru." Before Nado could respond, the police officer caught up and ordered the boy to empty his begging bag. Out rolled the three mangos he had stolen from the vendor. The cop pulled him from behind Nado and led him back to the vendor, whacking him on the shoulders a few times with his baton. "That story of Milarepa again," murmured Nado to himself. The old man squeezed next to him in the bus seat looked to see if Nado were talking to him. Nado had dreamed of the fable several nights during his convalescence at the hospital, and during his last few months there he had begun thinking of it in broader terms. Milarepa was not merely protecting animals from hunters. The broader moral was that the dharma offered all people refuge from their torments, whether inflicted by external events or their own minds.

The end of the freight train finally passed through the crossing and the bus started off. The bus conductor continued down the aisle, collecting tickets and looking for other rubes from whom he might swindle a few rupees. He saw Nado's Bhutanese face and approached him, but then, seeing his red robes, placed his palms together and said "*Namaskar guru.*"

"Namaskar," said Nado. He gave him his ticket.

"You are going to Siliguri?" asked the conductor in Hindi.

"Yes, and then all the way to Dharamsala."

102

"Ah, Dharamsala. It is very far away. You must change buses at Siliguri, you know. Get off there and wait for me, guru. I will tell you the way."

The conductor's new-found courtesy amused Nado. He did not deliberately intend to tease him, but the remark seemed appropriate: "Lord Buddha said each of us must find his own way."

A confused look came over the conductor's face. After a few seconds he waggled his head and said, "Yes, that's true. *Danyabaad*, guru." He then continued down the aisle. The bus soon pulled into the bus station, where Nado bought a roti for lunch, and transferred to the bus to Patna, and on across Bihar and Uttar Pradesh towards Dharamsala.

Three months later Nado found himself back in Thimphu. He had received a telegram in Dharamsala that his sick brother had died. The next day he arranged leave from the school and returned to Bhutan to arrange the funeral puja. While in the city, he had met Kencho, who drove him to see his new house and insisted that Nado accept 5,000 rupees from him as a donation to help cover the costs of the puja. The body had been cremated in Geylegphug, but Nado arranged for the prayers to be said at Dorjedra. Buying the food for the six days of feasts, supervising the cooking and the decoration of the altars, meeting his family members at the bus station, arranging their lodging, and all the other necessary tasks made him too busy to participate in the chanting of the prayers. He was too busy, really, even to think much about his brother's death, or the unexpected twists of his own life during the past year. But after lunch on the last day, after his family had gone home and there were no more arrangements to oversee, he slipped into the monastery's temple to listen to the final prayers. He sat against the wall beside the door, underneath the

103

smoke-blackened mural of Milarepa, and absorbed the sound and smell and sight of the ritual.

The fragrance of cedar smoke curling from the cluster of incense sticks on the altar brought his mind back to one and another of the thirty or forty prayer rituals he had chanted during the eight years he had lived at the monastery. He gazed at the altar's flickering butter lamps and the faded yellow and blue and red silk banners hanging from the beams. His eyes drifted to the side altar, where his father had propped up his brother's carpenter tools and his mother had left a basket of cookies and fruit and zow. He felt a bit surprised that he did not feel the intense sadness and loss that he had expected to feel over his brother's death. Ugyen was gone, that was all. His wife and child had moved in with her sister's family and were doing all right.

Sunlight brightening the room turned his gaze to the back window. The rain clouds above Talakha peak had drifted apart for a moment and a few afternoon sun beams were angling through the window. A yellow strip glowed on the chant leader's shoulder and the cymbals and polished pine floor boards in their path. He noticed that the window pane had cracked—and had not been replaced—during the time that he had been away. He focused on the prayer chanting and, recognizing the point in the sequence of the ritual, found himself mouthing the words silently. The low nasal tones washed back and forth between the rows of chanters, swelling in volume and tempo as the tempo of the drums increased, then settling back softer and slower again, over and over, until the gradual decrescendo of the almost inhumanly low final tone. Then he smiled at his own excited anticipation of the crashing of cymbals and concussive booming of horns that he knew would come next.

In October the next year, two foreigners who were working with government agencies in the capital strayed from a trail while hiking in the mountains above the Thimphu Valley. The track they were following became thinner and thinner and finally threaded out into a series of exposed ledges. Just as they were turning around to go back, they noticed a small wall of rocks and mud, with a window and door in it, built into an overhang of a ledge. They approached to examine it, but seeing a faint plume of smoke coming from a gap near the top, they stopped.

"Someone's at home," one said.

"Yeh," replied the other. "Let's leave him be." As they retraced their steps, a man in a monk's maroon robes opened the door and in English said, "Good morning. Please, come."

The surprised hikers stammered that they didn't want to disturb his privacy, but the monk insisted that they stay to visit.

They sat on the ledge outside the hermitage while butter tea heated on the tiny clay stove inside. Below their feet lay the forested mountainside and the golden ripe paddy of the valley's farms. On all sides above them were ridges of craggy peaks, their tops already snow-covered. The monk wanted to know who the foreigners were and what kind of work they did in Thimphu. He asked detailed questions, and they were impressed how well-informed he was about their projects in rural sanitation and education. He in turn answered their questions about what he was doing here, how he got his food, how long he planned to stay. He was in retreat, to meditate for three years and three months, a goal that many monks try to achieve at some point in their life. He had been here about one year already. Novice monks from Dorjedra monastery, lower down the mountain below his hermitage, brought up food a few times a week. There was plenty of fire wood for cooking and he had two good blankets to keep him warm at night.

He passed around a basket of zow and kept refilling their cups with tea, ignoring their polite protests until the thermos flask was empty. His name was Nado, he said, and no, he almost never found it lonely up here. There was a certain poetry, he said, to the view of the valley and mountain peaks, the sound of the wind rising and falling, the rain blowing up the valley, spattering down, then moving on, and the movements of the sun and clouds throughout the day. This kept him company and inspired him.

In His Majesty's Civil Service

By mid-morning, a few hundred people had streamed down the hill to Changlimethang, Thimphu's sports grounds along the river. Winston thought that Changlimethang, the site where His Majesty's great great grandfather's warriors slaughtered a rival warlord, was a fitting place for sports competitions. It was Sunday, the second day of the final match of the autumn traditional bow archery tournament. After the shooting on Saturday, the Ministry of Communication's team trailed the Druk Air Corporation Team 7 to 10. Druk Air had surprised nearly everyone by advancing even one round through the knockout tournament. Later, the fans were amazed (and several lost bets) when Druk Air squeaked by the Royal Bhutan Army's team in the semi-finals. Winston figured it was just beginner's luck: Druk would choke in the finals against the Ministry of Communication's veteran team. Still, Druk Air had some impressive shooters, ringers who probably had signed on with a promise of a free round-trip ticket to Bangkok or someplace. But Winston was not worried much. MinComm's team would wear them down in the end. He stood behind the target and gazed at the crowd. Only a few people were sitting in the ornate VIP pavilion. From where he stood, with the sun in his eyes, he could not make out who they were. Too early for most of the big shots to arrive, he decided. But there already was a large crowd of regular people sitting on the grass on either side of the 140 meter shooting range. Children were running and playing on the sidelines while brass-tipped cane arrows whizzed overhead. Adults chatted with neighbors and friends, jumping up now and again to retrieve toddlers who had wandered onto the range, and cheering when arrows thocked into the plate-size wooden targets.

Winston was a civil servant of the Royal Government of Bhutan, Administrative Cadre Grade 8, currently posted with the Ministry of Communication in the Public Works Department. MinComm was one of the biggest ministries in the government. Since it included the post office, telecomm, public works, urban planning, and a few other government departments which did not quite fit in any other ministry, it had a large pool of men from which to pick its archery team. Winston was an alternate on this fall's traditional bow team. During MinComm's first match, against the Bank of Bhutan, he had replaced one of the regular archers who had to show a Japanese consultant some microwave repeating stations out in eastern Bhutan. (A nuisance, but since the Japanese had financed the system, MinComm could not exactly tell their consultant to wait a week.) But after the regular man returned, Winston was not needed for the final match. Being an alternate galled him a bit—he thought that he was better than one or two of the regular team members—but for the sake of the team and the Ministry, he swallowed his pride and helped out on the sidelines. Besides, he reminded himself, the traditional bow tournament was not really his game. His specialty was the compound bow tournament, held in the springtime. Hitting a target with the cane arrows and bamboo bows of the 19th Century warlords' armies required strength and finesse, but the machine-like accuracy and power of a modern carbon-fiber compound tension bow and sleek aluminum arrows was Winston's thrill.

Winston spent most of the morning with the team. When Druk Air was shooting, he and the other MinComm players stood in front of their target and shouted taunts to distract their aim. Only at the last second, when the arrow was already in the air, did they jump aside. Most of the taunting was standard, tame stuff—that the shooter was hungover, or should have spent more time practicing than chasing after junior high school girls, that kind of thing. But they also shouted innuendo about some juicy gossip that was going around about one of Druk's players, which definitely embarrassed him and affected his concentration. On the other hand, when one of their own teammates was shooting, they stood behind him and cheered encouragement, and danced a jig and sang if he hit the target. As the morning wore on, Winston retired to supervise luncheon preparations. Two drivers from the office had built a campfire at the end of the sports ground and were cutting up chilies and pork and cauliflower for the ministry officials' and the team's luncheon. When Winston walked over to check on them, they had a huge vat of rice and the pots of curry simmering nicely.

"Kuzuzampo sir," they bowed when he walked over.

Winston nodded. "Everything under control?"

"Yes *la*. Everything is fine."

"Good," said Winston. "We'll serve luncheon at noon." He handed a tea thermos to one driver. "Here Dunbar, serve tea for the *dashos* and the guests. Remember, serve the dashos first, then the deputy directors, and so forth."

Dunbar waggled his head in agreement.

"Karma," he said to the other, "get the case of soft drinks from the Hilux and serve those too." Satisfied with

109

the preparations, he paused for a moment to retighten the cloth belt of his new, red and yellow plaid *gho* robe, then walked to the team's tent to chat with his office colleagues and watch the match.

At lunchtime MinComm led 17 to 14. The PWD director congratulated the team as they returned to the tent. After the directors, the deputy directors, and the guests were served (the minister was dining in the VIP pavilion), Winston and his family helped themselves and sat on the ground outside.

"Do you know who I saw your cousin's wife talking with just now?" his wife Tshering asked.

Winston sucked in his breath to cool off the hot chili peppers in his mouth. "Who?"

"Karma."

"Which Karma?"

"You know, Karma. Works in your office."

"The driver?"

"No, not the driver. *Sarchopa* guy, from Tashigang. Married to the Nepali woman—you know, the teacher."

"Oh yes. Karma Dorji. Talking?"

"Talking, smiling, . . . more than friendly, it seemed to me."

"Hmmm," said Winston, and arched his eyebrows. Tshering is a terrible gossip, he thought to himself, but better being married to a gossipy woman than to be in the dark about what his friends and colleagues were doing.

By midafternoon, the crowds' tea thermoses and bottles of Dragon Rum were empty and children were fussing to go home. Hot sun, alcohol, and the afternoon wind took their toll on the archers' aim, so at four o'clock, the day ended at MinComm 19, Druk Air 20. On Monday morning, Winston and several of his colleagues signed in at the office but then headed back to the sports grounds. Druk Air started out strong and MinComm just never caught up; by eleven thirty they had won the tournament, 25 to 21. "None

110

of us ever expected to get beaten by a new team like Druk Air," Winston explained back at the office. "It's almost like in the old days when a team would get a lama to put a jinx on the other. Since lunch time yesterday, we barely could hit anything and they just couldn't miss."

A high overcast had drifted over the thin winter sun when Winston returned to his flat at lunch time. He lived in the Public Works Colony, one of the largest housing complexes for civil servants in Thimphu. He had managed to get the lease for the flat several years ago, but had since transferred it to his wife. The government deducted one third of a lessee's salary as rent, so since Tshering was only a Grade 14 clerk, they saved money by putting the lease in her name. A raw northern wind swept swirls of dust into the grimy entrance way as Winston trudged up the stairs to his flat. He had to side-step around his neighbor's fire wood pile and duck under strings of yak meat jerky, which Tshering's mother was drying in the second floor landing. It was the fifteenth of the month, an auspicious day on the Bhutanese calendar, so his mother-in-law would spend the day praying and gossiping with her elderly friends at the temple. Tshering, he knew, would eat at her office's canteen, and the children would be at school. Winston would have the flat to himself for an hour of peace and quiet, which was just what he wanted this afternoon.

He filled a bowl of rice from the pot on the stove and poured himself a glass of Bhutan Mist whiskey. He usually did not drink during the day, but today it seemed appealing and, besides, by himself, in the privacy of his home, he could drink whatever he pleased without caring what others thought about him. He plopped down on a low, upholstered bench in their sitting room with a loud sigh and distractedly balled up a few handfuls of rice and popped them into his mouth. He glanced at the photo of His Majesty Jigme Singye Wangchuck, the *Druk Gyalpo*, the

111

King of Bhutan, which hung on the wall, and it reminded him of his meeting at the Ministry that morning.

He had arrived ten minutes late and was dreading the thought of walking in on the director while the meeting was in session. To arrive at a meeting after the highest ranking person was very bad form, contrary to the *driglam namzha* national etiquette guidelines which all civil servants are required to learn.

"Is Dasho in yet?" he had asked the director's secretary.

"No, not yet. The others are here though," she said. "By the way, how are you feeling today?"

"Excuse me?"

"You were sick yesterday, weren't you?"

"Yes . . . " Winston paused to think. He had taken the previous afternoon off to have a somewhat embarrassing medical condition treated at the hospital, but had not told anyone at the office about it. So how had she known? He barely knew her. "How did you know that, if I may ask?"

"Oh, my husband's cousin is a nurse at the hospital," she answered cheerfully. "I hope you're feeling better this morning."

"I see. Yes, much better." He straightened the back pleats of his gho and went into the conference room.

He greeted the other men and women at the table and took an empty seat. He adjusted his *kabne*—the plain white, raw silk shawl which driglam namzha required all men of common rank to wear in government buildings and official functions—over his knees, which was proper form when in the presence of a dasho. While he adjusted it he noticed how neatly and well the young woman sitting across the table wore hers. Women's kabnes were simpler affairs, red scarves with religious designs woven in, nothing all that fancy, but she managed to drape hers from her shoulder in an uncommonly graceful way. Winston did not

112

know what this meeting was supposed to be about: as usual, no one had distributed an agenda. He was about to ask the man seated next to him when the director walked in. All stood up respectfully while he took a seat at the head of the table, under the room's portrait of His Majesty, then they sat down and waited while he adjusted his red dasho rank kabne.

Dasho had spent the first half of the meeting getting briefings by the officials from urban planning and public works about various projects being run under those departments of MinComm. Winston was not involved with them, so he let his mind wander. Who was the attractive woman who wore her kabne so well? He had never seen her at the MinComm building before. She did look familiar, though. Maybe he had seen her at the vegetable market or at a shop or some place. Before he knew it, the woman was briefing Dasho on her project to change the official spellings of villages and other place names in the southern part of the country from Nepali-sounding spellings to Dzongkha-sounding ones. For example, she told Dasho, the Chirang District would henceforth be spelled Tsirang. She would coordinate with PWD to make sure that the "more appropriate" (as she called it) new spellings were used in road signs and all its maps and documents. What a stupid waste of effort, Winston remembered thinking. Her type really got on his nerves: so perky, so positive about any and all government policies, impeccably dressed in a gorgeous traditional *kira* and wearing a button with His Majesty's picture on it. She was even holding her hand coyly in front of her mouth as she spoke, which technically was driglam namzha for speaking to a high-level superior, but in this day and age was overdoing it. He would bet twenty rupees that she was just toadying to Dasho, making a good impression to advance her status in the civil service. He despised that kind of self-promotion, but honestly, who could really blame her for wanting to advance? And she was just so attractive and charming. Just watching her had tightened his throat and groin and made him sigh.

When the woman had finished her report, the office peon served tea. Everyone waited until Dasho had taken his first sip of the sugary, soapy-colored tea and then they felt free to drink their own and get up to stretch.

B.B. Giri, a colleague from urban planning, came over to say hello. "So, I heard you were at the hospital yesterday," he said. "I hope you're feeling O.K. and it was nothing serious."

"Oh, no, nothing at all, just a check-up," said Winston.

B.B. had said he was glad to hear it.

He had a good idea who B.B.'s source was: the neighbor in the flat above his was B.B.'s cousin. "It is impossible to keep anything secret in this country," he muttered to himself. He took a gulp of the Bhutan Mist. He snorted and winced as it hit his stomach, but then smiled and relaxed as heat radiated up to his brain. For the first time in over a week, he had an hour or so to relax all alone by himself. The thought came to him that he had not written in his diary for over a month, so he went to the bedroom and took the book from his locked drawer. He had had the diary for years but seldom wrote in it; it was really more of a journal of his thoughts than a diary. It gratified him to see his own words written in his own hand on the gray sheets of Indian foolscap. Flipping through the pages of the last several months it struck him that most of his entries were complaints about certain people or circumstances at work, things that he would not want to say in public, but which somehow made him feel better if he could unload in his diary. He decided that this time he should write something more positive, but his mind kept returning to the charming woman at the meeting. He was trying to refocus his thoughts when a knock on the door made him jump. *"Jhidaa,"* he whispered, and slid the book under the bench.

It was Durga Giri, from upstairs. She had heard footsteps in Winston's flat and thought that Tshering was home. She explained to Winston that she was taking a day off from work to wait for a plumber. Her kitchen sink was backed up and the National Properties Department had agreed to send a plumber over to fix it. She hoped that the plumber would arrive soon, so that she did not have to take tomorrow off as well. "Sorry I can't help you," Winston said, trying to mask his irritation. "I don't know anything about plumbing." When he returned to his diary, he found that he was no longer in the mood to write, so he locked it up and watched part of a Hindi movie video until it was time to return to the office. The video was a scratched and fuzzy bootleg copy, so badly produced that the blurred images of the tops of the heads of the audience in the cinema where it was pirated blocked the bottom of the screen. He had watched it so often that he was now bored of it. If only I could get down to Bangkok, or even just New Delhi sometime, he thought to himself as he switched off the VCR and gulped the rest of his Bhutan Mist. I could get some new videos, good American movies, not like the picked-over assortment of old Hindi flicks in the Thimphu shops.

Winston was the son of peasant farmers from Wangdi Phodrang District, the first from his village to ever go to college and join the government service. Winston's real name was Sangay Penjor, but ever since his college years at St. John's in Darjeeling, his friends had called him Winston. Most assumed that 'Winston' came from Winston Churchill. The real source, which nowadays he seldom told anyone, was that he and a roommate at St. John's had once gotten hold of a pack of Winston cigarettes from god-knows-where and smoked them. This had impressed his schoolmates and their nickname stuck. He graduated from

115

college with a B.S. in biology and planned a career in wild-life management or forestry, but when he joined the civil service, there was a greater need for administrators. Instead of a becoming a biologist, he entered the administration cadre, where his first posting was with the Ministry of Finance. That was ten years ago. Since then, he had been transferred to the Public Works Department of MinComm. It did not really matter so much to him any more where he worked; he liked the security of a government job and of course the chance to serve the king and the nation. He had been promoted two grade classifications since entering the service and hoped to retire as a deputy director or maybe even a director some day. This was an ambitious goal for a man from a farm village with no family connections, but not entirely unrealistic. Someday, he day-dreamed, he would drive around Thimphu in a government Land Cruiser just like the dashos.

His current job involved monitoring the costs of government construction contracts and approving contractor's invoices. He had never heard a reasonable explanation why all the construction contracts for the various ministries were routed through the Public Works Department. It was probably because PWD originally had the only engineering staff, although now each ministry seemed to have its own engineering unit. Ironically, Winston was not even an engineer. He simply approved the contractor payment reports that the field engineers from the various government departments submitted. The task which took most of his time was checking the field payment reports against the contractor's original bid estimates. If they they were within ten percent of the bid price, Winston approved them and sent them on to the Finance Ministry for payment. If the invoice exceeded ten percent of the bid, he had to contact the field engineers and the contractors to justify the discrepancy, then document the reasons and send them back to the various departments for approval.

116

The official policy, of course, was not to pay contrac-tors for significant cost overruns, except under circum-stances beyond their control. Sometimes, though, the government would award compensation for even fla-grantly irresponsible (in Winston's opinion) overruns. This was particularly prevalent when the contractor was a rela-tive or close friend of a high government official or the royal family, who would intercede on his behalf. This in turn (again in Winston's opinion) encouraged them to de-liberately underbid subsequent jobs. Most of the depart-ment directors understood the contractors' game, and over the years had talked about setting up policies to curb it. The issue had come to a head a few years ago when the former PWD director was reprimanded for detailing gov-ernment equipment to build a road to his home village. The new director then set up a review board to issue contractor licenses, keep records on each company's performance, and give preference to the best performers in future contract awards. As the secretary to the board, Winston processed all of its paperwork.

When he returned to his cubicle after lunch that day, his heart skipped a beat to find the deputy director of his unit rifling through the stack of paperwork on his desk. From long experience and his thorough training in driglam namzha, Winston instantly composed himself. The DD was a nice fellow, but his habit of snooping through his staff's desks really irritated Winston. Nevertheless, it was im-portant not to show annoyance or anger: people talked and before long one's reputation could suffer. "Good afternoon, sir," he said cheerfully, "may I help you?"

"Ah yes, Sangay, there you are. I got a call yesterday afternoon from *Ashi* Zam's secretary asking about a Class C contractor's license approval for Tandin Construction Company. It seems the owner is a friend of Her Highness and he's very impatient to get a license. I looked for you yesterday afternoon, where were you?"

Winston tried to sound as apologetic as possible. "Sorry sir, I had to be away from the office yesterday afternoon. It was for, um, some medical treatment. I . . . '

"Oh yes, I forgot about your boil," DD interrupted, "Hope it's all taken care of now. They can be painful."

Winston winced. He wanted to tell the DD that it was none of his business, but instead said, "Yes la, they can. I think it will be all right now, though. Thank you sir."

"Anyway, do you know anything about this license for Tandin?"

"Yes la, it's here in my file." He pulled the "Tandin Construction Co." file from his file drawer. "It is all set to go out, sir, but I needed Dasho's signature on the cover letter. He was out for the last two days. I hoped to get him to sign it this afternoon."

"I see," said DD. "Very good. I tell you what, give it to me and I'll get Dasho to sign the letter when I see him tomorrow morning."

Winston gave DD the license form and letter. "Thank you sir."

Winston stood by while the deputy director continued to rummage through the papers on his desk. DD picked up a sheet of paper and read it. "Is this your phone bill?" he asked.

Winston looked over DD's shoulder at the piece of paper. "Umm, yes it is."

"For the office or for your home phone?"

"My home phone sir. I have the bill sent here because we don't have a home post box, la."

"No, neither do we." DD scanned the list of calls. "Why did you call New Delhi?" he asked.

"New Delhi? Oh, yes. My wife's youngest brother is at university there. She called him about some family things."

"New Delhi, hmm. Must be a smart boy."

"Yes, la, very smart."

"Three hundred ten rupees for one call. Wow! Expensive, isn't it?"

"Yes, very expensive," answered Winston.

The DD put down the phone bill and waved the license approval form at Winston. "Glad you've taken care of this," he said. "Keep up the good work."

"Thank you, sir."

"Ah, Winston, may I join you?" asked P.V. Sharma, Winston's friend from the bridge design section of PWD. Winston was sitting by himself in the dingy canteen in the basement of the MinComm building, distractedly tracing patterns in some spilled rice on a grimy Formica table top with a spoon, when Sharma set his plate of rice and chilies down next to him. Winston had already finished a bowl of Maggi Instant Noodle Soup and was thinking about buying a few pakoras to chase it. Maggi was truly lousy soup, formulated by a Swiss multinational corporation and manufactured in cellophane packets by the millions in India. It was nothing but MSG and white flour: a poor excuse for Bhutanese noodle *thukpa*, but cheap and quick to prepare, so popular with office canteens like MinComm's. They chatted while Sharma ate, about each other's families and the prospects for the spring archery tournament. When Sharma finished, Winston ordered two whiskeys and a small plate of vegetable pakoras. Today was turning out to be one of those days when he did not have to be on his toes, but merely be at the office until five o'clock, so the idea of bunking off at the canteen with Sharma and a drink was appealing. He had scheduled a meeting with the district engineer in Paro at two o'clock, but then had to cancel it when the director commandeered the office vehicle and driver. The director's own government Land Cruiser was in the workshop today, or some such thing, and he could not be expected to drive his private car. As a result, most

119

of Winston's day was wasted, but it was something he had learned to live with and to expect now and then.

Sharma and Winston poured water in their whiskeys and sipped them. "Here's to the Army Welfare Project," toasted Sharma. Winston clinked his glass. "What would us simple folks do without it?" The Royal Bhutan Army's Welfare Project ran Bhutan's only legal liquor bottling plants, where it blended grain alcohol and various flavors into patriotic-sounding booze like "Dragon Rum" and "Bhutan Mist Whiskey", which were sold at affordable prices in nearly every tiny bar and village shop in the country.

Sharma smacked his lips. "Vile stuff," he said. "Have you ever drunk any good whiskey, Winston? Like Johnnie Walker or J&B?"

"No. How would I get it? It's only available at the government duty free shop, and only foreigners and the dashos can shop there."

"Oh, you could shop there too; anyone can if they pay in U.S. dollars."

Winston snorted. "Like I said, only foreigners and the dashos can get it."

"I drank some J&B once at a PWD reception for a U.N. project review mission," said Sharma. "At the Druk Hotel. Very nice. A completely different drink than good old Bhutan Mist. Try some sometime if you get a chance."

They munched pakoras and sipped their watered whiskeys. Sharma's comment about spending U.S. dollars made Winston think of his neighbor, who had recently bought a car. "Do you know my neighbor Karma?" he asked.

"The one from Tashigang that works in your section?"

"No, no, different one. Family is from Tongsa, I think. He lives in the Agriculture Colony, but just down the hill from my building."

"I don't think so. What about him?"

"Well, he bought a car last week. Or at least he started parking a car in front of his building."

"What kind?"

"Nothing fancy, a second hand Maruti."

"Still though, wonder where he got the money for that?"

"That's the thing. I'd like to know too. It probably cost him at least one *lakh*. Kind of a funny guy. Real quiet, doesn't talk much. Hard to know what he's thinking. He is a bit presumptuous to buy a car, don't you think? Like he wants to act like a dasho."

"Maybe, although a Maruti isn't exactly in the same league as a Land Cruiser." Sharma paused and shooed away some flies from the spilled rice on the table top. "Is the car registered?" he added.

"I guess."

"Well, then the police must have investigated to see where the money came from. You know, they always . . . "

"Hold on a minute," interrupted Winston. He lowered his voice and pointed over Sharma's shoulder. "Do you see that woman at the counter, buying a cup of tea?"

Sharma glanced back. "Yes. Dechen Tashi."

"Huh. Dechen Tashi. Does she work here?"

"Sometimes, why?"

"She was at a meeting I went to last Monday with the director, but I'd never seen her here before that. What is her job?"

Sharma explained that, as far as he knew, Dechen Tashi worked mainly as a translator with the Dzongkha Development Commission. It was the DDC's job to promote the Dzongkha language as the standard, national language of Bhutan. Even though it was the mother tongue of only about a quarter of Bhutan's people and far fewer could read and write it, it was the government's policy to enforce its use so as to promote national unity and preserve the

121

country's heritage. The idea was that English and Hindi brought too many foreign influences and were corrupting the traditional culture. Dzongkha was the language of western Bhutan, where historically the capital has been. But just as many Bhutanese spoke the south's Nepali or the east's Tshangla. At the office, most civil servants preferred speaking—and certainly writing—English. It was exasperating to translate official documents and reports from English to Dzongkha, only to end up translating them back again so that others could read them. But powerful people supported the DDC and it was considered unpatriotic to criticize its work. The previous summer DDC had ordered shopkeepers to replace the English writing on their shop signs with Dzongkha. Most complied only after DDC issued fines.

"At the meeting last week she was telling Dasho about the spelling changes for place names in the south," said Winston. "Has she done other projects for MinComm?"

"Sometimes she is assigned to MinComm to write press releases, policy statements, that sort of thing. In Dzongkha, of course."

"She must write Dzongkha well."

"Impeccably. And she writes English well too. You are familiar with MinComm's policy banning satellite dishes and cable TV in the country, I think?"

"Yeah," nodded Winston. "I read the editorial in the paper about it a while back. The usual stuff about decadent, materialistic Western influences subverting our spiritual culture and corrupting the morals of the youth."

"Yes. Well I heard that it was our Mrs. Dechen who actually ghost-wrote the editorial. She's a fast-riser in the civil service. She'll go far."

Winston glanced at her over Sharma's shoulder. Norbu, Winston's deputy director, had come into the canteen and she had bowed politely and was now smiling charmingly at whatever he was telling her. What a lovely, graceful woman, he thought. He gazed at her short-cropped, stylish haircut, her almond-shaped brown eyes, and her yet another beautiful, traditional kira, complete with a button of His Majesty. The perfect spokeswoman for MinComm and DDC. The big shots probably invite her to plenty of good whiskey receptions and do her all kinds of favors, he thought. Vague feelings of envy and resentment and lust crowded in together. He sighed. He wondered if she believed in half of the stuff that she had written in the satellite dish policy editorial. Wouldn't it just beat all if her editorial were just so many words to her, and in reality she owned lots of new videos and American music CDs!

Sharma followed Winston's gaze. "She's very attractive, isn't she?" he said.

"Yes, she is," murmured Winston. "Is she married?"

Sharma winked at him. "Lucky for her she is. Her husband's name is Ugyen, Ugyen Nyedup, I think. You'd never believe she has two children, would you?"

A few months later the deputy director summoned Winston into his office. "So, our team had bad luck in the compound bow tournament this spring," he said.

"Yes la, bad luck. The Army team was good this year. If we hadn't been seeded against them in the first round, I think we could have made it to the finals."

"Well, there's always next fall. You shot well though, I heard."

Of course I shot well, thought Winston; but he said, "Oh, not so well. I tried to do my part for the team."

"Yes, yes. And that's the important thing, isn't it?" DD rang his buzzer for the peon. "Tea?"

Winston declined politely.

The peon appeared and DD ordered two teas. DD shuffled through a stack of papers and finally found what

123

he was looking for. "Well, Sangay," he said, "I have good news for you. You were selected to go to AIT in Bangkok for a four-month training course."

Winston had no idea what Mr. Norbu was talking about. Perhaps he had confused him with someone else. "Um, me, sir?" "What sort of training?"

"Computer training. On a grant from the U.N. Development Programme. For, um . . . " (he scanned the document) " . . . ah, 'human resource development.' There were four slots and the director arranged one for PWD."

"You're not kidding, are you? They're really going to send me outside for training, la?" Winston could not quite believe it. To be sent "outside" to another country for training was a coveted perk for a civil servant. Even better, it looked great on one's record at promotion review time.

"Yes, that's what I'm trying to tell you," DD said. He was smiling as much as Winston was.

Winston thought for a second. "But why me? I don't do much with computers, you know."

"How long have you been in the civil service?"

"About ten years, la."

"And you haven't ever been sent for outside training before have you?"

"No."

"So, it's your turn to go. You're the most senior person on PWD's list of eligible candidates for training. It doesn't really matter whether you use computers or not."

The office peon brought tea. While they sipped it DD explained the program to Winston. Four months at the Asian Institute of Technology near Bangkok for instruction in office computer applications. He would be paid his regular salary plus airfare and the approved U.N. per diem rate for national civil servants. Of course, he was free to decline it, but that would be foolish. Winston did not have to be reminded of that. What incredibly good luck.

124

Winston spent the next two weeks filling out forms and going from office to office for a police security clearance and a passport. His wife checked with an astrologer, who determined that the departure date was auspicious for traveling. Friends kept coming over and giving him money to buy things for them at the department stores in Bangkok. He finally put his foot down when P.V. Sharma asked him to bring back a Sony video player. He felt guilty refusing, but that was just too much to carry back. The night before his departure Tshering threw a small farewell party at their flat and all his friends wished him well. Although they tried to hide it, Winston could sense their envy, and he took care to make little self-deprecating jokes, lest they think he had let the honor go to his head. He could not sleep that night. As he looked out the bus window at the familiar villages and paddy fields along the route to the airport at sunrise, he felt giddy, like a boy on an adventure.

At the airport, he was so excited that when he walked into the departure lounge and saw her sitting there, he became startled and confused. She was wearing a stylish, western-style dress! Outside the kingdom, Bhutanese were not required to wear the national costume, of course, so it was not unusual to see travelers on departing flights dressed in western outfits. He himself had brought along a few pair of trousers and shirts; but seeing her here, dressed like a foreigner, seemed impossible. Was this a dream? he thought to himself. It seemed more fantasy than real. Dechen Tashi saw him standing alone with a confused look on his face and cheerfully beckoned him over. She and the two men sitting next to her were the others being sent to the AIT computer training course. Winston joined them, taking a seat under the portrait of His Majesty, and chuckled to himself in amazement at his good fortune. It was his first ever trip on an airplane; he was even getting paid for it; and on top of it all he would have a chance to get to know this beautiful Dechen. The vague jealousy and disdain that

125

she aroused in him during the winter evaporated; all he felt now was excitement. Finally they gave the boarding announcement and they all walked across the runway to the plane. As the jet thrust up the runway and pushed his body against the seat back, Winston mumbled a short prayer of thanks for his good fortune.

Mr. Norbu, Winston's deputy director, closed his office door to read the file in private. It was Winston's confidential personnel file, which he had managed to borrow by pulling some strings at the Royal Civil Service Commission. DD had noticed a change in Sangay's (DD disliked that "Winston" nickname) attitude since he had returned from the training course in Bangkok and he thought that the file might explain it. For one thing, it seemed that Sangay had become sloppy with driglam namzha. He always wore his kabne and gho properly, of course, and was never disrespectful to his superiors. But his deference and politeness seemed perfunctory somehow, as if in his heart he despised driglam namzha and only followed it to keep up appearances. And then there was the unexpected memo that he sent to Dasho about requiring all contractors with government contracts to post performance bonds. It was not a bad idea, actually even a pretty good one, but the way he had handled it—just going ahead on his own and submitting a memo to the director himself without going up the usual chain of command—was so cheeky. Is that what he had learned in Bangkok, that etiquette and protocol were no longer important? It reminded DD of his own sixteen-year-old son's adolescent rebelliousness.

And another thing, thought DD. Sangay had quit MinComm's fall tournament archery team after a nasty little scene when the captain chose him as the alternate. There was nothing wrong with pride, of course, and Sangay's free time was his own, but it just seemed out of character. Before going to Bangkok he had been such a positive team player,

126

but when he got back something about him had changed. And finally, what about the second hand Toyota that he bought last month? Where the devil did he get the money for that . . . or the nerve to actually drive it around town like he was some kind of a big shot?

"**Mr. Sangay Penjor.** Born 1962 in Gaselo village, Wangdi Phodrang Dzongkhag," the RCSC personnel file read. The DD scanned past Winston's biographical material: "Married, two children, . . . ;" he knew all of that already and skipped to the last page. "Ah, here we are," he said to himself, "the most recent entry."

"Computer applications training course at Asian Institute of Technology, Bangkok, Thailand, June—September, 1995. Funded under UNDP HRD grant No. BHU / HRD / 6-93. Satisfactorily completed four-month course of study; eligible for merit increase commensurate with training. While at course drew full salary entitlement plus U.S.$50.00 per diem UNDP-approved living allowance for national civil servants.
Comments: Sources reported that while at the training assignment, Mr. Sangay Penjor apparently had an amorous relation with Mrs. Dechen Tashi, a government civil servant posted with the Dzongkha Development Commission, who was also assigned to complete the same training course at that time. Sources further reported that Mr. Sangay and Mrs. Dechen shared the same room at a student boarding house during the course. In his expense reports Mr. Sangay made no reference to this arrangement, nor offered to refund any portion of the UNDP-approved per diem due to savings resulting from it, if any."

DD closed the file and took a deep breath. "I see," he said softly to himself. "At least we know where he got the money for his car."

They lay together under two blankets on a rickety bed in the bare hotel room. Frozen white moonlight cast

127

their shadows on the concrete wall. Winston had driven from Thimphu to Paro that morning to check contractors' bids for the Paro Junior High School renovation contract. Dechen had caught the afternoon bus over, with some similar work pretext to keep her there overnight. They had eaten dinner and had drinks at a better hotel but Winston had recognized another of the customers there, a district official whom he knew, so they decided to avoid gossip and get a room somewhere else. This hotel, the 'Sonam Rinchen', was a dive, but at least no one there knew them.

Winston had joked as he unfastened the clasps of her kira that she wore her button of His Majesty the King even to their out-of-town trysts. Yes, she always wore it, she had replied. It was like her kira and kabne, and bowing to superiors, part of her uniform as a civil servant. They made love and afterwards dozed off, but later were wakened by a barrage of barking by Paro's stray dogs as the full moon rose above the ridge. Winston thought again now about Dechen's reply, and did not want to let it drop.

"I really don't understand you," he said. "In Bangkok, you loved being able to wear whatever you wanted and watch TV and read all those foreign magazines. I never once saw you bow or suck up to anyone."

"That's right. And I liked not having to be constantly thinking about what other people would say about me, about making them jealous or suspicious and all that."

"But then you came back and put on your old 'uniform', as you call it, as if nothing had changed. Bowing and covering your mouth with your kabne and all the rest of driglam namzha, and writing about protecting our national values from satellite TV and western materialism. It's . . . inconsistent. Doesn't that bother you?"

"No. It was easy for me to put my uniform back on. I think it's important. We're a small country and it's important to keep our culture intact."

Winston lay looking at the ceiling. "That's what they all say, from His Majesty on down. But do you really think that our culture is so fragile that it would all of a sudden disappear if we were allowed to watch 'CNN' and 'Star TV' or look a dasho in the eye instead of bowing and mumbling 'yes la' all the time?"

Dechen snuggled against him. "Sangay la, whether or not you follow driglam namzha won't break our culture. But it would certainly ah, dilute it. Then we'd start being just a variation on every other little third world country. Consumer junk and Hindi flicks from India, the crassest of American pop culture, with maybe a few unique Buddhist quirks here and there to keep it interesting for tourists."

"It's changing now anyway. We teach all the school children to read English and people like us get sent outside for training: do they think we will still behave like our grandparents did, tending the cows and groveling to the wealthy families and lamas? Don't you think it's demeaning?"

"Ehh," said Dechen, "so that's your real problem. You think it's demeaning that royal family members can have satellite TV, and that dashos can drive Land Cruisers, but you can't."

"Well, don't you?"

"TV and nice cars and prestige don't equal dignity, Winston. If you feel proud of yourself and confident that you're an intelligent and good person, why should the fact that wealthy people have more privileges than you be demeaning? We have our families and our jobs where we can serve the country. For me, showing respect to privileged people is not demeaning."

Winston did not like being lectured to and said, more to irritate Dechen than to mean it, "so it's O.K. to act like a sheep as long as you don't believe you're a sheep."

Dechen rolled over. She would not normally bother arguing with Winston when he got worked up like this, but in the back of her mind, she thought he was foolish enough to get himself in trouble over so small a thing as his pride. "Look, I get afraid for you sometimes," she said. "That kind of attitude will just gnaw at you and get you into trouble. You begin to act disrespectful at the office and antagonize people or make them suspicious, and . . . "

"I don't act disrespectful," he cut in. "I always wear my kabne and I stand when Dasho comes in and all that."

"Maybe you do, but only half-heartedly. I've seen you. You think it's enough to just go through the motions, but it's not. You must sincerely believe in driglam namzha."

"All right, next time I see our director being chauffeured around in his land cruiser I will prostrate myself on the ground in front of him."

"You will only get yourself run over. And look, since we're talking about this, take that Toyota you bought. You should be more discrete with it."

"Why?"

"Because . . . "

"Because only people who are at the deputy director level or above are supposed to have Toyotas? I bought the car with my own money and there's no rule saying I can't drive it!"

"Yes, I know, but you drive around and people get envious and think you're trying to set yourself on a level above them. Like they say, nails that stick up get pounded down. It makes me nervous for you."

Winston didn't respond. He knew she always got the last word. He stroked her shoulders and back in silence for a moment. "Does your husband know that you see me?" he asked.

"I don't know," answered Dechen. "I don't ask him. Just like he doesn't ask me whether I know about his mistress. We get along well enough that way, I guess." She paused and snuggled against his shoulder. "Does your wife know about me?" she asked.

130

"She must, I guess."

"Does she . . ."

"Shh, what was that?" Winston whispered. He sat up in the bed. "I heard someone outside in the hall."

They listened: at first there was nothing but dogs barking and night silence. Then there was a soft tread of footsteps in the hallway, and a door opening.

"Must be going to the toilet," Dechen whispered.

A little later, they heard someone clearing his throat and howking. "Yes," Winston said, "just going to the toilet."

They lay silent while the moon rose above the eaves and its silvery beams faded from the window; he was snoring when she fell asleep.

It was at Thimphu's sports complex a few weeks later that the police picked Winston up. He was there with his son and daughter to watch the high school basketball tournament. He remembered noticing a young patrolman from the security detail watching him on and off throughout the afternoon. As he was steering his children through the crowd in the lobby after the last game, the patrolman and an older officer motioned for him to stop and pulled him aside. It all happened so quickly and quietly that Winston doubted anyone else had noticed it.

The older officer led them into the ticket booth and closed the door. "Your identification card, please," he said.

"I'm sorry, officer, I don't have it with me just now," Winston apologized. Of course I don't, he thought. No one carries their ID card around Thimphu. This cop knows that.

"No ID. What is your name please?"

They probably know my name already too, Winston thought. He recognized the older one, Dorji somebody; if he knew Officer Dorji, Officer Dorji no doubt knew him. "Sangay Penjor, he said. I live here in Thimphu, at the PWD housing colony.

"You're a civil servant?"

131

"Yes."

"Mr. Sangay, the reason I stopped you is because you are in a government building and you are not wearing national dress. You're a civil servant. Surely you know the driglam namzha rule about this."

Instead of a gho, Winston was wearing a sweater and the pair of Levi jeans that he had bought in Bangkok. He glanced at his five-year-old son, who was wearing sweat suit pants and a jacket. The children had frightened looks on their faces; the boy would probably start crying soon. Winston became angry. "But, it's only the sports complex, and on a Saturday afternoon," he sputtered.

"I'm sorry, but I have to issue you a fine." He took a pad of fine forms from his pocket and wrote one out. "The fine is five hundred *ngultrums*. Will you pay it now?"

"No. I won't," said Sangay sharply. "Pah! This is ridiculous. There were at least twenty other people watching the games who weren't wearing national dress. It's just the sports complex; it's not like it's the *dzong* for heaven's sake."

Winston's son began to whimper. The young patrolman fidgeted and looked embarrassed. Officer Dorji looked at the frightened little boy and he too began to get flustered. "I am just enforcing the rules Mr. Sangay. If you want to argue about it, you can talk with Lieutenant Tshering at the station on Monday morning."

"All right officer, I will do that." Winston snatched the fine slip from him, roughly grabbed his children's hands, and tugged them out the door of the ticket booth. Several people watched and murmured to each other as he marched his children out to the parking lot and put them in the car.

Winston was not getting anywhere with Lieutenant Tshering. The officer kept repeating that the sports complex was a public building, that the high school basketball tournament was a public event, and that the regulation said that all Bhutanese nationals were required to wear national dress in public. It did not matter whether twenty other people at the tournament on Saturday were wearing western-style clothes: Winston had broken the regulation and he must pay the fine.

Normally, Winston would have paid a fine without arguing. He respected the police and sympathized with them for having to do unpleasant duties sometimes. But singling out him for violating the dress code seemed so unfair that arguing with the lieutenant just made him more stubborn and more angry. Finally Lieutenant Tshering said that he had had enough of it. If Sangay refused to pay the fine, he could go to court and argue with the magistrate.

"I think I will just do that," said Winston.

The lieutenant took a drag on his cigarette, stroked his mustache, and slowly blew out the smoke. "All right, as you wish. But you know, of course, that the magistrate will ask to review your police record."

"That doesn't bother me. My police record is clean," said Winston.

"Would you like to check and make sure?" Lieutenant Tshering took a manila folder from a stack on his deck and handed it to Winston. "Sangay Penjor" was printed on its label.

Winston gasped softly and stared in disbelief. How did they know all of this, he wondered. They knew to the dollar what he had paid for his car and that he had saved it from his Bangkok per diem. They knew that he and Dechen had shared a room in the boarding house. Each of his out-of-town rendezvous with Dechen over the past three months was noted with dates, locations, and even summaries of some of their conversations. "Jhidaa," he murmured, they had even heard the conversation about driglam namzha that they had had at the hotel room in Paro. It was all there, written in the police file. He felt his heart racing and his stomach tightening in a knot.

"I . . . I've done nothing illegal," he stammered.

Lieutenant Tshering took back the file. "Except violating the national dress regulation at the sports complex on Saturday. Which really is a small matter, not worth presenting your file to a magistrate about, I think. Or the Royal Civil Service Commission either, no?

Winston stared at the floor.

Tshering leaned back in his chair and took another drag of his cigarette, then continued. "So, my friend Winston Cigarettes, this five hundred ngultrum fine is not just about wearing jeans to the basketball tournament. You pay the fine, you straighten out your attitude, and your police record doesn't leave this office. If not, you'll just be asking for problems down the line."

Winston knew that the matter had been settled for him. "Yes sir," he murmured. "Thank you la."

As the lieutenant wrote out a receipt for the fine payment, he said, "You know, I might as well tell you, your girlfriend handled this much more graciously than you did."

"Dechen?"

Tshering waggled his head. "She took our hint immediately and paid her fine."

"Well, she's smarter than I am, I guess," Winston said. He had meant the remark to sound casual and cheerful, but it came out strained. "What did you fine her for?" he asked. "She always wears the national dress."

"Oh, her . . . I believe she was apprehended dumping garbage into the drain next to her flat."

Winston involuntarily snorted a laugh.

"The public sanitation regulations are nothing to laugh about," said Lieutenant Tshering, with the slightest grin at the corner of his lips. "All right Mr. Sangay, you may go," he said, and held out his hand.

Winston clasped it and bowed slightly. "Kuzuzampo Lieutenant," he said. He was at his desk at the MinComm building in time for the morning tea break.

Sangay did not see much of Dechen after that. He telephoned her office a few times during the first week, but she did not return his calls. He met her once coming out of the canteen in the basement of the MinComm building, but she merely smiled blandly, said "Kuzuzampo Sangay" and continued walking out. Sangay was sad for the first few weeks that she avoided him, and several times considered forcing a meeting by going to her office. Eventually he decided that this would just embarrass both of them, so he began preoccupying himself with work and his family, and found that he thought about her less and less. When the weather got warmer he made amends with the captain of MinComm's archery team and got back on the squad for the spring compound bow tournament. It was during the first day of their second match, as he stood on the sidelines watching a teammate shoot, that the PWD director drove by on the road and stopped to watch. Sangay bowed politely and called out, "Kuzuzampo la dasho."

The director beckoned him over to his Land Cruiser. "Ah, Mr. Sangay. It's you. How are you? Is the team shooting well this spring?"

"Yes la dasho, very well," he said, bowing his head and cupping his hand in front of his mouth. "We will surely beat this team and advance to the finals, la."

"I'm glad to hear it," the director said. He sat in his car and watched an arrow whiz through the air and chunk into the ground next to the target. "Yes, I'm sure we will make the finals."

"Thank you dasho," said Sangay.

Dharma Robbery

Sonam took another pull off the dirty plastic jug of
ara and gazed morosely over the valley below him. By
squinting, he could clear his drunken fogginess enough to
make out the black speck of his camp down on the valley
floor. Further down the whitish meandering line of the
creek, the blue plastic tarp specks of the valley's other two
camps showed up more distinctly. At intervals, white
threads cascaded down the "U"-shaped valley walls, con-
necting the grey clouds to the creek by tiny plumes of mist.
When the wind fell, the soft rumble of the waterfalls drifted
up to his ears. Then the wind rose again and the snap whipping of frayed prayer flags on the rocky knob above him
blocked all other sounds. His brother Gempo sat next to
him, fumbling with the whet stone as he drunkenly sharp-
ened their chopping knife. After a while Gempo heaved
himself to his feet and stumbled to catch his balance. "Well,
he said, "the sooner we do it, the sooner it will be over."
They each picked up one end of the blanket-wrapped bundle and lugged it the last few meters up the rocky knob.

At the base of the whipping prayer flags, they untied the blanket and rolled out the bundle. Sonam fortified himself once more with ara, muttered a prayer, then took up the heavy, sharp knife. His first chop was wild and missed the corpse's knee joint, slicing into its calf instead. Shivering with revulsion he flailed again with the knife, hacking through the back tendons but missing the joint. He was hyperventilating and felt faint; even with ara-dulled senses, it was still horrible. A hand touched his back and he shouted and jumped. Gempo grabbed his arm and slurred, "Easy little brother. Think like you're butchering a yak." Sonam shut his eyes for a moment, then gazed at the whipping prayer flags and composed himself. Taking a deep breath, he grasped the corpse's leg with one hand and cleanly sliced through the joint with the other. He kicked the leg over to the side of the knoll, next to a prayer flag pole. Yes, just like butchering a yak, he thought to himself.

Doggedly focusing on this thought only, he cut more skillfully through the other knee. Two quick slices with the knife and he kicked the second leg aside. The ara was doing its work; the horrible task was getting easier. He then rolled the corpse over to sever its thighs from its pelvis. He tried not to notice, but there was the dead girl's little patch of pubic hair, and, as he feared, he began to feel aroused. He desperately clutched at composure, muttering "just like butchering a yak—it's not young Lhaden." Try as he might, as he hacked off one thigh and began chopping at the other, his eyes kept straying to the black triangle of hair, and nausea and shame congealed in his stomach. He fought down a vomit-tasting belch of ara and kept on, kicking the second thigh away and rolling the corpse back over to begin chopping through its spine. But when he kicked aside the lower half of the torso and intestines and stomach and greenish bloated guts slopped out, vomit surged to his throat and he heaved. He spun around and dropped to the ground, cradled his head in his arms, and moaned. He did not look up as Gempo picked up the knife, muttered a quick prayer, and finished severing the elbow and shoulder joints, and finally the girl's head.

The girl, Lhaden, had been the daughter of one of the other families who herded its yaks in the valley. Her death was so unexpected; she was only fourteen years old. She had had dysentery, but that was something that everyone suffered now and then. Then she got drenched while fetching in some yaks from up on the ridge in the rain, and came back to the tent shivering. A dry blanket and hot butter tea by the cooking fire did not seem to help much, and she kept shivering. She could not keep food in, but lay in a blanket coughing, moaning and feverish. After two days she was too weak even to crawl out of the hut to pass her watery, blood and mucous diarrhoea. She died silently sometime during the next night.

At their winter camp, where fire wood was plentiful, young Lhaden's family would have cremated her corpse. But at their summer grazing camp in this high valley along the Tibetan border, where there was barely enough monsoon-sogged willow and rhododendron shrub wood to keep a cooking fire going, a cremation pyre was impossible. So they resorted to a sky burial, the custom of poor families on Tibet's treeless plains, placing the corpse on a high promontory and chopping it up for the ravens and eagles to devour. If guided by the proper rituals and prayers (so the lamas taught, anyway) the consciousness was set free to find its next incarnation, while the corpse returned to its elements. The greatest lamas were said to be able to embrace disease, death, and all other aspects of life, and then detach themselves from them, knowing that they were illusions veiling the purer nature of reality. But for the yak herder families in the valley, the more immediate nature of reality—the weather, pasture, accidents, and sickness—were what mattered. And these were all affected by, if not ultimately controlled by, the local spirits. Funeral *pujas* were the monks' business, not poor yak herders'. Guidance towards a higher reincarnation would be nice, but the immediate reality for them was to destroy the corpse to drive away the evil spirits that infested it, pray that they did not return, and do what they could to relieve the deceased's family's grief. As good neighbors, Sonam and Gempo offered to take the family's burden and perform the burial, knowing that some day the favor would be returned in some way. But even for them it was a dreadful task, the horror of which even a jug of ara could not completely numb.

Pema had spent the afternoon churning yak butter. She was spooning it into a cured yak bladder when her big yak dog began jumping at its rope and barking ferociously outside. It must be Sonam and Gempo, she thought with relief. The clouds had lowered and it had begun to drizzle, and she had been worried that they would get caught out after dark. She listened to them mumbling a prayer to the little spirit catcher shrine, which she had set up near the corral to divert and ward off the evil spirits that had caused the girl's death. She mumbled the words of the mantra along with them. Sonam staggered coming down the entrance step, and grabbed the main roof pole to keep his balance.

"Finished?" she asked.

"Yes, finished."

The brothers settled down on the low rock bench along the hut's side wall and took off their soggy yak wool cloaks. "Horrible job," said Gempo.

Pema finished sewing the bladder of butter closed. "Yes, I am sure it was," she said. She put the bladder into a large storage basket, which hung from the roof pole to keep out mice. "Her family is still too crushed, they could not have done it." She swatted the young boy who sat near the fire pit. "Get more wood so that we can cook supper for uncle and father," she told him. The boy fetched willow branches and dried yak dung cakes from the wood pile. She turned to her husbands and said, "They told me to thank you. They said you gained much merit for it."

The branches were too big for the fire, so she borrowed Gempo's knife to cut them. The knife was a long, heavy blade made from a leaf spring of an old car, which they had bought several years ago at the bazaar in Punakha. They used to have two knives, but on the way to summer grazing camp back in May, Pema had somehow misplaced hers, which for them was a serious loss. She glanced at Gempo uncertainly as he handed it to her; he read her mind and said it was O.K., he had cleaned it after the sky burial. She split some of the branches, piled them on the embers, and blew, and soon homey-smelling willow smoke was billowing up to the roof and curling out the door opening. The hut consisted of a shallow, square pit dug into the ground with field stone walls built up to chest level on all sides. For a roof they pitched heavy, thickly woven yak wool tarps across roof poles, forming a peak in the center above the door and fire pit. Like the other two families in the valley, they had tried using new-style blue plastic tarps from India, but found that they disintegrated after two years of intense sunlight at the 4,300 meter elevation of their valley, so had gone back to using traditional yak wool tarps. Yak wool was heavy to carry and got waterlogged after a few days of rain, but it did not cost hundreds of rupees to replace every few years. Outside the hut was a corral area, where they staked and tethered those yaks that tended to wander off at night, and a pit with a board over it, which served as a latrine.

Pema soon had a pot of butter tea steaming. The buttery, salty broth cheered her husbands, and Gempo managed to tell an expurgated version of the sky burial to his nephew and niece, whose curiosity had overcome their mother's instructions not to ask. The drizzle had turned to

141

rain, which dripped through the tarp at its seams, but after a second bowl of turnip, chilli pepper, and yak milk stew, everyone's spirits rose. Pema told her daughter to turn on the radio and see if there was music. The little girl fetched the radio from a hanging storage basket, excited because they only played it on special occasions. No sound came from it though, and they decided that the batteries must be dead. It was discouraging: of the six batteries that they had brought to summer camp, all had died after only three or four hours of use. Even if they were the cheapest Indian batteries available, they were still expensive for a yak herder family. Normally, something like dead batteries would not bother Pema, but with the rain, the girl's death, and the evil spirits about, the silent radio dragged her down. Sensing his wife's discouragement, Sonam got up and fetched his *dramnyen*, a rough, three string lute, which he had carved years before. He played their favorite songs and they all sang half-heartedly. Outside, the clouds, dark, and loneliness of the remote valley closed in; but around the smoky fire, singing kept their minds off the fear and dread of the day. After some time they all curled up under blankets on the juniper bough bedding and fell asleep.

Pema had to cross the ridge a few weeks later to search for a yak which had wandered out of the valley. At the point where she reached the ridge line, she could see the sky burial site's rocky knob and prayer flags a few hundred meters to the south. Fortunately, there was no sign of the yak up there. Disposing of the dead was men's responsibility, so she had never been to a sky burial site. She imagined what they were like, and always avoided them. They were scary places, haunted with bones and evil spirits, which could interfere with a person's life if you gave them the chance. One death in the valley that summer was terrible enough; the last thing Pema wanted to do was to attract the spirits to her, too. On the other side of the

142

ridge, the slope dropped steeply through a thicket of mountain azalea and then loose shale talus into a rocky bowl, before descending out of site into the next valley. She scanned the bowl for a moment and, as she expected, at last saw her yak grazing by itself on a sparse grassy patch. By the time she thrashed through the azalea bushes and picked her way down the sliding talus, she was so irritated with the shaggy black beast that she threw a rock extra hard at it to get it moving back up. The yak trotted back up the slope further to the south of the route Pema had taken, and when she finally reached the ridge again, sweating and out of breath, there was the yak sitting on the ground just below the sky burial knoll.

She glanced at the frayed prayer flags flapping in the breeze up on the knoll. The wind chilled her sweaty back and made her shiver. She was determined to shoo the yak back down into her camp's valley and get away from this bad luck place as fast as possible. But as she stood there, catching her breath, a shiny white paper thing caught her eye. It was an empty packet of "Wujangs", Chinese-made cigarettes, crumpled up and left on the ground. Recently, too, by the look of it. How odd, she thought. As far as she knew, none of the people from the three camps in her valley smoked. Who had been up at the burial site then, she wondered. She picked up the cigarette packet and turned it in her hand with curiosity. She had only seen cigarettes a few times in her life. The thought of her mother, who had spent the last ten years of her life as a nun, and who had told her that smoking was a sin for Buddhists, came to mind. It fascinated her; she had a sudden urge to go up to the site and look around. But then she remembered how risky it was to attract the attention of evil spirits. Still, she was so curious . . . after a moment of hesitation, she took a breath, mumbled a mantra and tip-toed up the knoll.

It was ghastly. Arms, torso parts, legs were strewn about, partially decomposed, buzzing with flies and picked

143

over by birds. She gasped and slapped her hand over her nose against the stink. She knew she should leave immediately, but it was so morbidly fascinating that she could not pull herself away. Then after a few seconds, she realized that something about the carnage seemed odd. She couldn't quite decide what it was. And then it came to her. The head was missing. And the thighs were gone too. That was enough, the place was haunted for sure. She shuddered, took a quick last gaze, and hurried down to where the yak was sitting. She and the yak were half way back down the ridge to the valley before her heart stopped racing.

Later, when she had tethered the yak in the corral, she told Gempo and Sonam about the missing body parts. Gempo decided that a snow leopard must have raided the site and dragged the parts off. This made sense to Pema, but she could not help thinking about the sight all day. Who dropped the cigarette package up there, if no one in the valley smoked? And, come to think of it, why would a leopard take only the head and thigh pieces? There were evil spirits at that place for sure, and the last thing she wanted was to get involved with them. It was just as well to leave the site alone to the birds and leopards and spirits. That evening she chanted extra prayers to the spirit shrine to keep her family safe; but she dreamed in her sleep of the pieces of corpse rotting up on the desolate knoll, and knew that the spirits would not let the bones rest in peace.

October came, and with it the frosty nights and gorgeous sunny warm middays that signalled the time to move down to their winter camp. The last of the monsoon rains had brought snow to the ridge tops and mountain peaks, and before long the bright blue gentians and magenta primula in the valley would freeze and die. Three or four small bands of Himalayan blue sheep, which Pema sometimes saw grazing up on the ridges during the summer, had descended to the slopes just above the valley floor.

The skittish animals formed up into a herd of forty or fifty, which spooked and ran when a person came within a few hundred meters. They grazed the thin grass and stunted heath that the yaks left behind on the lower slopes, moving up with the sun in the day and back down at night, watching nervously for leopards above and people below, waiting for the yaks to depart, so they could reclaim what was left of the valley's grass before winter set in.

The day that they shifted from summer camp down to winter camp was one of the holidays of their year. The children buzzed with excitement when Gempo told them that tomorrow would be the day. That afternoon Sonam and Gempo had taken the dog and herded in all the yaks and staked them in the corral. They woke before dawn the next day and made one final breakfast of tea and buckwheat cakes, then all set to breaking down the camp. Moving camp was never a complicated affair: in less than an hour, the roof was down, the wood pile covered over, and their belongings packed up. Their pots, blankets and the rest of their household gear was stuffed into four large pack baskets and tied to wooden saddles on two of the biggest yaks. The roof tarps were rolled up and tied onto a third. Two more yaks were loaded with the baskets of the summer's produce: about thirty kilograms of butter—ten bladders full—and two dozen strings of *chogo*, rock hard cubes of cheese. The five calves that had been born in the spring were all healthy and fat and in good shape to survive the winter.

Gempo and Sonam pulled down the roof poles and stowed them, disturbing a nest of field mice in one of the post holes in the process. Pema placed the spirit catcher shrine with the rest of the summer's scant trash in the fire pit and watched for a moment while the smoldering breakfast embers flared up, consumed it, then died away 'til next year. Before the sun had risen above the ridge, their herd was on its way to winter camp. Pema and the children

145

walked half-way back in the herd, shouting and shagging pebbles at any yak that stopped to graze or that wandered away. Sonam walked ahead and at the rear of the herd Gempo and the dog walked sweep. At the point where the trail left their valley to switch-back down a headwall into a lower one, Pema stopped for a rest and admired the view. Ahead and above loomed Masang Gang and Teri Gang, brilliant in the crystal blue sky, with morning sunlight flashing pure white off their fluted glaciers, which somehow hung weightless from the peaks' near-vertical south faces. As the morning heated up, a few wispy clouds rose from a lower valley, crossing Pema's line of sight, two thousand meters below the brilliant peaks. She hugged her son and daughter and sighed at the magnificent sight, while the yaks plodded down the switch-backs, oblivious to it all.

The children especially liked winter camp. The site was in a sunny meadow in a forest near one of the tributaries of the Mo Chhu River. Unlike the wind-stunted scrub of the high summer valley, its forest had plenty of fir and poplar and birch trees, so fire wood gathering never took very long. The yaks seldom wandered far from the meadow and did not have to be milked often, so the children could devote most of the day to play. Their warm hut had a wood plank floor, tight rock walls, and split fir slabs for a roof. They even had a wooden door to keep the wind out, and could slide a slab over the smoke hole when it stormed. They spent hours each day playing with the children of one of the summer valley families, who had its hut nearby. Sometimes Pema or Sonam or Gempo took them into Laya, where they had cousins and there were over a hundred people to see and talk to. And their older half-brother, uncle Gempo's son, came and stayed with them for the three months of his school vacation.

Soon after they had settled in, Gempo decided that he would take two yaks and a load of cheese and butter down to Punakha. The yaks would be butchered, and he

146

would sell or trade the meat and dairy for rice, tea, batteries, new clothes, and other essentials. One thing about Punakha, of which Gempo was well aware, was that it usually required some delicate arrangements for slaughtering yaks. Punakha was a religious town, Bhutan's historic capital, where the monk body still kept its winter headquarters, and one had to be circumspect about killing animals there. Of course, once the animals were dead, there were no religious rules against butchering and eating the meat, so he could count on getting a good price for it at Punakha's bazaar. Arranging their deaths was the tricky part. Killing sentient beings, including yaks, was against Buddhist teachings, which Gempo himself tried—at least technically—never to break. But there were several indirect methods of promoting a yak's demise, which even most monks would wink at. Stampeding it towards a cliff was a good one, since, after all, it was the yak's own choice to jump or not. But, as far as he knew, there were no high cliffs within easy distance of Punakha's bazaar. Gempo decided that the best arrangement would be to find a non-religious man or a Moslem or Hindu who was willing to slaughter the yaks; the person's small fee was worth it to avoid any possible risks to his own karma. If all else failed, he would get drunk and do it himself, and blame it on the ara, but he doubted that that would be necessary.

On his way down the Mo Chhu River trail he calculated what he could get for the meat and dairy. If he made good deals, he should have enough to buy the essentials, some betel nut, a few bottles of cheap whiskey, and some sweets for the children. Plus, as he promised, a new chopping knife for Pema (the old one had not been left behind at winter camp, as they had hoped). He hoped there would still be enough to hire a pony man to pack the load back to their camp. If not, he could pack it all on his back. He could reach Punakha in three day's walking, but there was no sense in hurrying a yak, so four would be better. He would stop over one night in Gasa, the district headquarters town, on the way and visit his son at the government school there. A day or two in Punakha, seeing the *dzong* and temples and all the cars and trucks, selling the yaks and shopping. There would certainly be dice games to join in at the bars. Maybe he would be lucky and hitch a ride back to the end of the road on a farm tractor or a road crew truck, then find a pony man on the way up the river. He thought of a pony man named Tshewang, from Damji village, whom he had met a few times on the Mo Chhu trail. He had traded some chogo with him for a pack of cigarettes earlier in the summer, and made up his mind to save a string of the hard yak cheese cubes in case he ran into Tshewang again. One long day from the road head back to Gasa (where he could certainly eat a supper and breakfast with the school children for free), and then another long day back to winter camp. Nine, maybe ten days total. He was enjoying the trip already.

A few days after Gempo left, Pema decided to go on a trading trip of her own. She had not been to Laya village since the spring, and always enjoyed seeing the nice houses there and talking with her cousins and other women whom she knew. In addition to trading fresh gossip, she might also get some winter supplies. The Laya people grew potatos and turnips and buck wheat, and some of the men from time to time crossed the passes into Tibet and brought back Chinese goods. They were usually happy to trade with herders like Pema for butter and cheese at a lower rate than what she would pay for Indian stuff in the shops in Punakha. Last year her cousins had introduced her to a woman named Kinley Dolma, who had given her a good deal on Chinese sneakers. Kinley was a proud woman, who lived in a big house, and Pema had felt self-conscious and nervous around her, but even so she decided that it be worth it to check in with her again. The next day at dawn, she packed a bladder of butter and some strings of chogo onto a yak, took the children, and set off for Laya.

It was a fun walk that morning. They had surprised two musk deer feeding in the forest and the children laughed as the deer bolted down the steep mountainside. Crossing a shoulder where herders had burned off the forest floor and killed the trees a few years back, she noticed that some people had been up there recently cutting the dead trees and dragging away the logs. Near the burn area, Pema knew a little side track, which led ten minutes around the mountain shoulder to an exposed spur with a magnificent view of Masang Gang. It was one of her favorite spots. Long ago a little *chorten* had been built there. Chortens were small shrines with four white-washed stone walls and a peaked flag stone roof. A broad red strip was always painted at the top of the walls, just under the roof line. Walking clockwise around a chorten gained a person religious merit and brought good luck for a journey. Sponsoring the construction of a chorten, though, gained far greater merit, which could be compounded by sealing precious stones, jewelry, or valuable religious items inside, or commissioning a slate carving of Lord Buddha or *Guru Rimpoche* or some other saint to be built into the wall. As far as Pema knew, she and her family were the only ones who remembered that the chorten was there. It seemed very old; the roof stones were covered with moss and lichen. She figured that the family who had built it had long ago died out or forgotten about it.

It was not only the magnificent view that drew Pema to the chorten, it was also a sentimental place for her, full of memories of her mother. Her mother had been a yak herder woman like herself, but had put on a red religious robe and become a nun after the children had grown. After she died, Pema had placed a *tsa tsa* of her mother on the little ledge below the chorten's roof. A tsa tsa was a small

149

cone made from a mixture of a deceased relative's cremation ashes and clay, which was stamped with mantra symbols and fired, then painted an auspicious color. Since her
mother's death, whenever Pema passed by on the trail, she
detoured to the chorten and made it a little ritual of cutting
away encroaching brush and weeds or replacing fallen roof
stones. Once she had even whitewashed the walls. As she
picked her way along the overgrown track to the site on
this day, she suddenly remembered that it was at the chorten that she had left her knife, during her last visit on the
way to summer grazing camp.

She simply could not believe her eyes. The front wall
of the chorten had been broken open, its white stones
strewn on the ground. Horrified, she peered into the cavity.
It was empty. No religious items or precious stones; the
vital innards of the chorten were gone. She was dazed; she
simply could not believe her eyes. Even in her imagination,
she could not conceive of a chorten desecrated in this way.
Sometimes naughty teenagers would write their boy-
friend's or girlfriends' names on them, but to chop one
open—it was almost like murdering a person. She stood
rigidly, staring at the gaping hole until finally her daughter
timidly said, "*Ama*, who did this?"

"They must have been drunk to chop apart a chorten," she muttered. "How else could a person do this?"
Her little boy sniffled in fright. She grabbed their hands
and pulled them toward her. "Let's get away from here,"
she whispered, "there are evil spirits here now. She tugged
the yak's rope and hustled them all back up the path.

An hour below Laya they crossed a side creek and
passed by an army outpost. A few soldiers and women
strangers were washing clothes in the creek. Several other
soldiers were playing a game with a white ball, slapping it
back and forth over a net. Pema was preoccupied by the
dreadful image of the ruined chorten and wanted to get to
Laya as soon as possible, but the children begged her to let

150

them stop and watch. The game fascinated the children. Her son could not take his eyes off the white ball. All the soldiers were wearing strange western style shirts and pants decorated with green and brown leaf-like patterns. On one side were Indians, darker-skinned people whom, Pema knew, the children had never encountered before. They were speaking a language that she could not understand. The Indians, she noticed, seemed to hit the ball back more often than the shorter Bhutanese men on the other side, who seemed to spend more time chasing it and laughing at each other. Pema felt a bit shy, standing beside the path with her yak and two children, but none of the players seemed to pay any attention to them. After a few minutes she too became distracted by the game. She did not notice the two men coming down the path until they were right next to her.

"Kuzuzampo ama, doing some trading today?"

She flinched and whirled around to face a Bhutanese officer, a tough looking little man with a mustache and cocky smile. Her heart was racing from the surprise. "Yes la," she replied, and forced herself to return his smile. The other, a tall Sikh with a graying beard and maroon turban, also smiled and nodded. He sniffed the air, scrinched his nose, and gazed at her yak. She noticed that he had a gold tooth.

"They're both smoking cigarettes," whispered Pema's daughter.

"Chh!" Pema hissed. She could tell that the Bhutanese officer understood. "We are just going to Laya, sir," she said, and bowed.

"I see," he said, and they both continued on. After the two officers had passed by, she took a deep breath to calm herself, then swatted the children and shooed them along the trail. The image of the crumpled cigarette pack flitted through her mind.

151

The trail broke out of the forest into Laya's lowest farm terraces and climbed towards the village between stone-fenced potato and buckwheat fields. The fields were fallow after the harvest and yaks and pigs had been turned loose to graze the stubble. As they hiked up towards the houses, they caught up with two girls, who were hauling heavy loads of firewood on their backs. Laya girls and women wore heavy black wool robes, cinched at the waist, with white borders woven with orange and red crosses. While in the fields, they wore striped aprons to protect their robes, in Tibetan style. They liked to wear necklaces of turquoise and coral beads, as many as they could afford. But their most distinctive fashion was their conical wicker hats, woven from bamboo splints, with a little stupa shape at the top, which they lined with waterproof gut to keep out the rain and strung strings of tiny turquoise and coral beads from the back. Like the *Layapa* women, Pema wore a black wool robe, but seldom bothered wearing a hat. And she could never afford to buy the kind of jewelry they wore. As they passed by the first cluster of wood-timbered and mud-plastered houses, they met one of Pema's cousins. Within a few moments, happy greetings and sharing of family news forced her dread of the ruined chorten to the back of her mind. Kinley Dolma was at her house, the cousin said, and she thought that she had some goods to trade. With a promise to spend the night with her cousin, Pema let her children go off to play and led her yak up the path towards Kinley's.

Kinley must have the biggest house in Laya, thought Pema. She scanned the pile of firewood stacked against the courtyard wall and decided that it would last her own family for three winters. Two ferocious-looking dogs bounded out as she tied the yak to a stake, snarling fiercely just out of the yak's kicking range. She called up to the second floor windows and a woman's head poked out—it was Kinley. Kinley looked down at her for a second or two with a frown, as if deciding whether to invite her in, then her glance fixed on the yak and the pack baskets, and she smiled and beckoned Pema up. As Pema climbed the steep log ladder from the windowless barn up to the family's living quarters, she noticed what looked like bins full of potatoes and turnips along the walls. The thought of how tenuous her own family's food supply was from year to year went through her mind. Kinley met her at the ladder entrance. Even in the dark entry way, Pema could not help noticing that she was wearing at least three coral and turquoise necklaces.

"Have you come to trade some butter?" asked the stout, older woman in a cheerful voice.

"Yes la," answered Pema. Her eyes still had not adjusted to the dim light.

Kinley glanced at her for a moment. "You are Pema, from up past Rodophu, no?"

"Yes, I traded some butter with you last year," answered Pema.

"Yes, yes, I remember. Please sit and have some tea." Kinley glanced back to a young woman who was sitting near the stove. "Tea and *zow*," she said quietly, then turned back to Pema. Pema watched the young woman get up and set a basket of roasted rice snack in front of them. Probably her daughter, Pema thought.

"So how is your family," Kinley was saying, "Did you have a good summer up at your high camp?"

"Oh, yes, my family is fine. We had a pretty good summer; alot of rain, you know."

The daughter brought a pot of steaming butter tea and waited for Pema to fumble her cup out of her robe pouch.

"Yes, so much rain. Much of our potato and turnip crop rotted in the field. It will be a lean winter for us, I fear," said Kinley. "I'm happy that you are doing so well, though."

153

Pema remembered the bins of food by the ladder, but decided she must have been mistaken in the dark. She felt a little embarrassed and mumbled, "I'm sorry." Kinley made a sad face and shrugged, which flustered Pema, so she tried to change the subject. "Did any of the village men get over to Tibet this summer?"

"Yes," answered Kinley, "but you know, with the rain, there just weren't many days that they could cross the passes, so only a few trips were made. What to do?" She laughed lightly, then touched Pema's arm and lowered her voice. "Trading with the Chinese is not a very profitable business, you know. Sometimes I wonder if it's even worth it at all."

Kinley made Pema nervous, but she tried not to let it bother her. The butter tea was excellent, and she had not eaten any zow since last spring. She gazed around the room. Hanging from a beam near the window Kinley had at least six or seven hammered aluminum ladles. Nice ones. And hanging on the wall were five of the most gorgeous copper pots and pans that Pema had ever seen. She glanced at her own shabby herder's clothes and felt self-conscious. Kinley must be the wealthiest woman in Laya, she thought.

"Here, I have something you'll be interested in," Kinley said, and got up and went to a trunk. She brought back some paper cards and a red rubber thing. "These are some pictures of Lhasa, which I got from a trader. This one is the Potala, and this one is the Jokhang."

Pema took the postcards of the holy city and bowed, touching her forehead to them. The Potala and Jokhang were magical names to her. She had heard about them, that they had been magnificent huge buildings full of sacred relics and images and gold and incense. The Dalai Lamas and other high lamas had lived there or meditated there. She had heard stories from her parents that even people from Bhutan used to go on pilgrimages to these places, used to bring their crippled or sick children and relatives

154

there to be cured. The pictures confused her: she had heard that the Chinese had destroyed these buildings, but here they were, with buses and crowds of people in the foreground.

Kinley sensed her confusion. "Of course," she said, "they are not the same as they used to be. The Chinese fixed them up, rebuilt walls and repainted them for tourists to see. But they are mostly empty shells now. They stole all the images and gold and jewels and artwork long ago, the despicable robbers." Pema gazed at the postcards in silence, impressed at how much Kinley knew about the holy city.

"Anyway," said Kinley, "here's something that is happier. My trader friend bought this in Lhasa too."

"What is it?"

"Watch. You blow it up like this, then you sit on it . . . like this!" The cheap, Shanghai-made whoopie cushion farted loudly. Pema burst out laughing, completely forgetting her shyness in this wealthy woman's house. Kinley laughed too, very pleased with herself. "You try it," she told Pema. Pema carefully blew it up and then sat gently on it. The air fizzed out. "No, you have to really SIT on it, hard!" laughed Kinley. This time it worked. A big, loud fart. They both laughed some more. Pema wished she could show it to her husbands.

As they talked, the early afternoon sunshine began slanting into the window. Pema noticed how one warm ray fell on Kinley and illuminated her necklaces and jewelry. They were gorgeous. One necklace was large blocky balls of turquoise and red coral set apart with finely worked silver beads. Another alternated lozenges of amber with lapis lazuli. The silver broaches which pinned her dress together were massive and finely worked. But the piece which struck her the most with admiration and envy was a single large *zee*, a zebra-striped agate, which she wore on a silver cord. Zees were rare stones with auspicious power.

A mother who owned one would pass it on to her daughter for generations. Very wealthy or very religious people sometimes offered a zee to be sealed inside a new chorten as an act of great merit "The poor chorten," whispered Pema.

"Pardon?" interrupted Kinley.

"Oh, nothing," The image of the gutted chorten was so disturbing to that she did not want to mention it.

Kinley slowly stood up from her mat. "Well, you came here to trade some butter and cheese, no? Let's go down and see what you've brought."

They went down to the yard where Pema had left her pack baskets. Kinley beckoned for her daughter to join them. They agreed to trade the butter for a basket of potatoes and a basket of turnips. Kinley said it was a sacrifice for her, that the harvest had been bad and there wasn't much potatoes or turnips to spare, but Pema had got a good look at the storage bins this time, and really did not believe her. They went back upstairs with the strings of cheese.

"What did you have in mind for the chogo?" Kinley asked.

"I'm not sure what you have. Do you have any sneakers, or the red plastic boots for the children?"

"I think I may have a few," nodded Kinley. "What sizes?"

Pema did not know anything about sizes. The sneakers were for herself, Sonam, Gempo, and her and Gempo's ten year old son. The boots were for the four and seven year old. Kinley unlocked the padlocked door of her storeroom and went inside. "Yes, I have a few sneakers and boots." Pema peeked into the dark room and watched Kinley rummage under a large tarp. "Are blue boots all right? I don't have any red ones," she called out. Blue ones were O.K. She brought out four pair of thin soled, green sneakers and two small pair of cheap plastic boots. Pema's pair fit

156

well, and she decided that the sizes were about right for the others.

Kinley re-locked the storeroom. "So, we are all set," she said, smiling.

Pema stood for a moment awkwardly.

"Yes?" said Kinley, "is there something else?"

"Well . . . I . . . " Pema was embarrassed. "I thought that I could get a few more things for five strings of chogo, that's all."

Kinley put a look on her face that seemed to Pema to be surprise and hurt. "Well, it is expensive for me to get these nice shoes from Tibet, you know, especially this summer with such bad weather for traveling." Pema now sensed a tone of embarrassment coming into Kinley's voice, and she felt even more awkward. "But I certainly don't want you to think that you didn't get a good bargain." She turned around and said to her daughter, "Puchu, do you think that five strings of chogo is worth six pairs of shoes?"

Puchu answered shyly, "yes mother."

Pema said softly, looking at the ground, "But the children's boots are very small ones."

Kinley stood still for a moment, then nodded. "Yes, I suppose they are. That Puchu is too hard a bargainer. Not like her soft mother." She gave a quick laugh. "Well, let's see what else we have that might make you happy." While Kinley reopened the storeroom and rummaged around, Pema caught a look of what seemed to be embarrassment in Puchu's glance. Kinley brought out five packets of "Wu-jang" cigarettes. "Do your husbands smoke?" she asked.

"No," Pema said, sheepishly. "May I look inside to see what you have?" She stepped in through the door as Kinley put the cigarettes back. Before Kinley could throw the tarp back over the box, Pema saw that it was full of cigarette packets. Hundreds of them. She was amazed. Kinley stood up and blocked her view of the room. "Um, do you have any cooking pots?" Pema asked.

157

They agreed on an aluminum pot, with a lid thrown in for free, and Pema felt much better about the trade.

As she was packing the baskets onto her yak out in the yard, the image of the box full of cigarette packets again reminded her of the crumpled Wujang packet at the sky burial site. "Do you know, Kinley la," she said, "we had to do a sky burial for the child of a family at our grazing camp who died this summer."

"Yes," said Kinley, "The poor girl. A tragedy. We heard about it. So very sad for her family."

"But later, the strangest thing happened," Pema went on. "I checked at the site a few weeks later and some of the parts of the corpse were missing."

"Ugh! Those grave robbers are despicable."

"Beg pardon?"

"The grave robbers. They sell the heads and legs of corpses for the skull cap and thigh bones, to be used in monastery rituals. They have no respect for the dead."

Pema's mind raced. She remembered visiting a temple one time and seeing the ritual items made from human bones: flutes made out of thigh bones, skull cap drums and bowls. She had heard that items made from the bones of teenage boys and girls were the most powerful and valuable. "That's barbaric!"

Kinley-lifted her hands and sighed.

"I just don't understand how a person could . . . who would do such a thing?" Pema's blurted angrily.

"Very bad people," Kinley said. "They aren't local people. They're outsiders—low life from other districts, maybe Chinese or Indian soldiers, foreigners. They sell them to certain monks who know the rituals for extracting the bones, or to collectors from Thimphu who arrange it all. Eventually, you know, they fetch high prices at monasteries in Kathmandu or India or maybe even Tibet. These outside people—they have no decency. They do anything for money."

Pema was overwhelmed. She shook her head and muttered, "what is wrong with people these days? And we thought it was a leopard up there that disturbed the corpse."

Kinley gazed at Pema for an instant with a look of disbelief, then quickly turned away. "Well, I hadn't thought of that," she said. "Of course you may be right. It could just as well have been a leopard. Come to think of it, it's probably more likely, isn't it?"

As Pema led her yak down the path to her cousin's house, Kinley calculated the profit she might make from selling the cheese and butter in Punakha. Even after the pony man's fee for carrying it, she figured, she still should be able to clear 290 or 300 rupees. Oh, yes, there were also the potatoes and turnips. Well, 250 rupees then. Not bad.

Pema and the children returned to winter camp the next morning. She hustled the children past the army outpost, not letting them stop to watch the volleyball game. This time she was less curious of the soldiers than suspicious. They were intimidating, especially the Indian ones. She noticed that several were lounging around and smoking. It all gave her the spooks. On the trail up towards the burned-over shoulder, she made up her mind to go back to the gutted chorten and have another look around. For one thing, in her shock the day before, she had forgotten to look for her knife. For another, she felt a strange desire to look for some clues about who might have done it. What kind of clues, and what she would do if she found some, she did not know. But, as at the sky burial knoll, a morbid fascination drew her.

She was thinking of this when her daughter, who had strayed ahead, ran back in a fright. Around a bend came two young soldiers, bent over and sweating under the weight of large bundles of firewood on their backs. Pema started in surprise, then tugged her yak aside to let them by. They smiled cheerfully and nodded to her as they passed. Her heart was pounding. Could it be that soldiers like those two not only broke into the chorten but also took the pieces of the corpse? She had thought about it the night before and it seemed to make sense: what Kinley had told her, the tall Sikh with the gold tooth, the cigarettes. It definitely made sense. A soldier could easily take a few bones and a zee down to Thimphu or India when he went on leave. The soldiers were replaced by new ones every six months or so, and she doubted that their packs were ever searched when they left. All of a sudden she was convinced; she had to tell Sonam. She hurried the children and the yak along. At the side trail to the chorten, she remembered her knife, but the thought of the evil which infested the place made her shiver. To hell with the knife, she decided. Gempo had promised to buy another one anyway.

"The dasho in Gasa should know about this," she told Sonam. She had been awake off and on all night thinking about the chorten theft and the grave robbers. Sonam had argued that they were just ignorant yak herders and it was not their business to get involved with crimes like this. But she was four years older than he and he knew from experience how hard it was to make her change her mind. It was outrageous, after all, and if it would make Pema feel better by going all the way down to Gasa to talk with the district administrator, she should go. He would take care of the children while she was gone. And besides, he agreed, it would be a good chance for her to see her son at the school. But she should not go alone, it was never good to do anything alone. She said that she would probably meet someone on the trail to walk with, and maybe would meet Gempo on his way back from Punakha. She set off alone at dawn the next day.

On the trail south down the Mo Chhu River she fell in with two Layapa girls. Their parents had taken them out of school for a week to help with fall chores, and now they

160

were returning to the Gasa school. They wore school uniforms, cotton kiras like southern town women wear, not the wool robes and aprons of their village. They knew Pema's son and giggled when she asked them questions about him. At a place where the river rapids cut into the cliff and the trail switch-backed up and over the gorge, they met a pony man who was waiting for his thin horse to pick its way slowly down. He was hauling rice to the army camp below Laya, he told them. Pema said that she was going to Gasa to visit her son. (Perhaps she was overreacting and being foolish to go speak with the district administrator, she thought. The pony man need not know about that.) The man said that he took a load up to Laya about once every month or so, except in winter when snow blocked the trail. She told him about her family, how they herded yaks and where their camps were. The pony man said his name was Tshewang and that he thought that he knew her husband.

"I think he was the one. He said that he and his brother herded yaks in a valley above Rodophu and had a family there. Very nice man, generous. He's done a little trading with me now and then, once just this past summer."

"I don't think it was my husband," Pema said. "He tells me about everyone he meets and I'm sure he's never mentioned you."

"Well, it must be someone else then," said the man.

The skinny horse plodded down the last switch-back. Pema asked, "Did he tell you his name?"

"I guess, but I can't remember it," he said.

"Gempo? Sonam?"

"Maybe it was Gempo, come to think of it."

"He's never mentioned you," she said.

The pony man shrugged, then walked on with his horse. "Must have been someone else," he called back. "Have a safe trip."

161

Pema had a delightful day, listening to the school girls' stories about Laya and the Gasa school, and telling them in turn about her life as a yak herder. The hours and distance flew by unnoticed. The last part of the trail climbed over a side ridge, far above the river canyon, then wound half way back down again to Gasa village. From far off Pema spied Gasa Dzong, the district citadel, built massively into a bluff that commanded the view of the neat farm-houses, terraced rice paddies, and wheat fields sloping down from its base. Far below, the jungled walls of the Mo Chhu valley stretched away into the southern haze. Pema had been coming down to Gasa once or twice a year since her oldest son had started school, and the view of the lush, hazy jungle and neat orchards and fields never failed to impress her. It was so much softer and richer than the cloud-cloaked mountain meadows and talus slope ridges of the high country. A cuckoo sang lazily somewhere off in the jungle. The farmers had already harvested their rice and set loose their cattle to graze the paddy stubble; brush fences piled around the conical stacks of rice straw kept the cows from eating their winter fodder. Above Gasa Dzong rose the mountain that the locals called Little Jho-molhari, little snow goddess, its peak and steep ridges covered with autumn snow that already glowed pink in the late afternoon light.

Smoke from cooking fires was spreading in a wispy lens over the ramshackle houses and shops in the bazaar as she and the girls trudged into the village. Several dogs intercepted them, shattering the cool evening stillness with barking, as they climbed the hillside past the army barracks and government health clinic to the school. The students were lining up for their supper of rice and curry as they arrived, so Pema took a place in the line behind her son. After dark she rolled up in her blanket on the school's play field and rehearsed her speech to the dasho. She decided to stick to the chorten robbery and not to say anything

162

about the disturbed corpse at the sky burial site. As far as she knew, none of the summer valley families had reported the girl's death to the police, so it would probably be best to avoid possible complications in this regard. After some time she fell asleep, with Orion and his earth dog chorus to keep her company.

She walked up the stone steps to the dzong's outer courtyard early the next morning, before the fog had burned off from the jungle in the valley below. No one was around, so she killed time by walking around the base of the fortress, admiring how its masonry had been fitted into the ledge and boulders of the bluff, as if it grew naturally from them. Doves and swallows flew in and out of their roosts between the wood-shingled eaves and the massive whitewashed walls. Later, a caretaker arrived, and she told him that she wanted to see the dasho.

"Which dasho?" he asked.

She didn't know. She told him the story of the robbed chorten.

He decided that she should report the robbery to Gasa's police captain and explained that the dzong offices did not open until nine o'clock. Her puzzled look told him that clock time meant nothing to her, so he promised to take her to the captain's office when he arrived. He looked at her rough woolen dress and sneakers. "Don't you have a kabne?" he asked. "You must wear one inside the dzong."

No, she did not own one.

"O.K. no problem. I'll borrow one for you."

She thanked the caretaker for his kindness and waited the next hour until officials and townspeople began arriving for the day's work.

The caretaker led her through the massive wooden doors and up a dark stone stairway into an inner courtyard. Off the courtyard, passageways led to the offices of the

163

district's secular officials—the district administrator, the officers for education, health, agriculture, and the rest—and the magistrate's courtroom. Another wide stairway continued up to an upper courtyard, carved into the side of the bluff, from which radiated the quarters, offices, and temples of Gasa'a *dratshang*, the district's monk body. The caretaker left her in the lower courtyard and went to search for the police chief. A quarter hour later, he returned to tell her that the captain had gone down to Punakha and would not be back until tomorrow or the next day. She could come back then. She apologetically explained that she came all the way from beyond Laya and her children were back at her camp and wasn't there anyone else she could talk to? The caretaker thought that perhaps the *dasho dzongda*, the district administrator, would be willing to speak with her. "Come up and sit in the foyer outside his office," he told her, "and I will try to make an appointment for you."

She sat all morning while officials with stylish *ghos*, shiny leather shoes, and clean kabnes came and went. She felt awkward in her own dirty and smoke-blackened clothes and edged into the shadow at the end of the bench. At one point a young agriculture official struck up a conversation with her while he waited for his appointment. At first she felt too shy to say much, but when he began asking her detailed questions about the condition of the pasture in her valley that summer, she became animated and chattered at length about her herd. She noticed other people sniffing and grinning, so she laughed lightly too. Later, another man, a health official maybe, started asking her if her children had been immunized. She did not understand what he was talking about so told him "yes." He started to question her further, but was then summoned into the dzongda's office. Finally, she was the last one left in the foyer and her stomach was growling for lunch. She decided that everyone had forgotten about her and had made up her mind to leave when a young woman appeared and ushered her inside.

Pema stood in the doorway for a moment, half hiding herself with the door curtain, and took in the sight of the office. The dzongda sat at a large desk under the window. On one wall hung old shields and swords and a portrait of the *Gyalpo*, the king; colorful woven tapestries hung on others and covered a sofa in the corner. A white fluorescent light bulb buzzed at the ceiling. After a moment the dasho looked up and motioned for her to enter. She bowed low and hesitated at the doorway; he chuckled and insisted that she sit down. She shuffled in with her shoulders and head bowed, holding the ends of her kabne out in front as the caretaker had shown her. She had never seen a chair like this, with a black plastic seat and shiny metal legs. She sat in it shyly.

"My secretary tells me that you want to report a robbery from a chorten," he said.

"Yes la dasho."

He sniffed the air and turned to open the window behind him. "Why didn't you report it to the police?"

Pema looked down at the floor. "I'm sorry dasho, but they told me the captain is not here now."

He thought for a few seconds. "Ah yes, that's true. Well, since you are here, why don't you tell me about this robbery. Where it was, when it happened, that kind of thing."

She told him all about the chorten, how she tended it, how she thought that no one else knew about it, then how shocked she was to see it broken open and empty. The dzongda asked her to speak slowly and clearly; he was from another part of Bhutan and had trouble understanding her Laya yak herder's dialect. While she spoke, he spit betel nut juice into a cup and wrote a few notes on a pad. His teeth were stained red. He explained to her how the

165

government of Bhutan treated chorten robberies very seriously. Over the years, he said, a great many of Nepal's and Tibet's chortens and temples had been broken into to supply an illegal trade in religious art objects. Selfish, wealthy foreigners paid large sums of money for the zees and other temple offerings. The situation was not so bad in Bhutan yet, but the number of robberies was growing by the year. The government usually sentenced convicted chorten robbers to life in prison. Unfortunately, the government could not arrest and punish the foreign collectors.

"Do you have any idea who may have done it?," he asked Pema.

"It's the soldiers, la. Or maybe the blond foreigners with the colorful tents and cameras."

The dzongda spit into his cup and sighed. "Did you actually see soldiers or trekkers robbing your chorten?"

No, Pema had not.

"I don't think soldiers or trekking groups are the ones who break into remote chortens in the mountains," he said. "I think that it is local people, who know where the chortens are. We've seen cases where soldiers or trekkers have bought zees or religious items from local people, but they aren't the ones who rob them." He gazed out the window for a moment, then turned to her. "Why do you think that it is the foreigners and soldiers?"

"Kinley Dolma, a smart Layapa lady, told me," answered Pema.

Dasho leaned back in his chair. "Ehh, Kinley Dolma, the famous smuggler of Laya. Do you do business with her?"

Pema sensed some sort of a trap. "Um, no dasho, but she's a wealthy woman, la, and everyone near Laya knows her."

"I'm sure they do." He spit in his cup again. Let me give you some advice, Ama . . . what is your good name please?"

166

"Pema, sir"

"Let me give you some advice Pema. I wouldn't do any trading with Kinley Dolma if I were you. We have a law against smuggling, did you know that? With only a few policemen and a few small army outposts for the whole district, it's difficult to catch smugglers in the act, but we have heard plenty of stories about her. She is a sharp operator, with a reputation for . . . how shall I say, driving too hard a bargain with good simple people like yourself. If I had to make a guess about who is behind zee trafficking from robbed chortens in Gasa District, I wouldn't discount our friend Kinley."

A shiver went up Pema's spine, but she tried not to change her expression.

Dasho noticed her nervousness and quickly added, "But of course right now I have no evidence of this."

Pema was thinking about the handsome zee on Kinley's necklace. She wondered whether she should mention this, but just wearing a zee did not prove that she stole it. Besides, it was important to keep on good terms with people whom you know, and tattling on Kinley Dolma would surely lead to trouble. "Yes dasho," was all that she said.

"By the way, Pema, since we're on the subject, you wouldn't have heard any stories about people disturbing sky burial sites, would you? People taking bones and selling them, or anything like that?

Pema bit her lip. "Umm . . . no dasho."

"Well, just a thought. Listen, I'd like you to do something for me and for the government, all right?"

Pema nodded.

"If you see anything or hear anything about anyone robbing chortens or burial sites, or selling or even just having stolen zees, or bones, or other religious items, you will report it to the police, all right? If you can't come down to Gasa, you can tell the health worker at the Laya clinic. He is a good man and you can trust him. Will you do that?"

Pema nodded. "Yes la."

"All right then, Pema. You may go. It was good of you to come all the way down here to tell me."

Pema stood up and backed out of the door, bowing.

No one else was walking up to the north the next morning, and Gempo was not expected through for a few days, but Pema decided to go by herself anyway. She stopped for lunch at a place called Koina, where a small river rushed out of a side canyon into the Mo Chhu. It was a muddy, wet place, but there was grass for ponies and a rock hut where travelers could make a fire and get out of the rain. Smoke was seeping out of the roof hole and a thin horse was tethered outside. She ducked in and, when her vision adjusted to the dim light, was surprised to meet Tshewang, the pony man whom she met on her trip down. He was cooking rice and tea and offered to share the lunch. While the rice cooked, she asked him whom he knew in Laya. He said he knew several of the families there.

"Do you know Kinley Dolma?" she asked.

He seemed to hesitate for a second, then said that sure he knew her; that everybody knew Kinley. He had carried a load for her now and then in the past, but if he could help it, he preferred hauling for other farmers. Kinley was too stingy, always trying to get a lower price. How did she know Kinley, he asked. Oh, as he said, everyone knew Kinley Dolma.

After eating, they both took naps. Waking before he did, Pema decided to return his favor by packing up his lunch things and carrying the pack baskets outside. As she lifted the lid off one of the baskets to put in the cook pot she glanced inside and . . . there inside were dozens of packs of Wujangs. And a bladder of yak butter . . . her butter! She was sure of it. She gasped out loud, and the pony man stirred. She stuffed in the cook pot and sack of rice and

168

crammed down the lid, and before he was fully awake, was lugging the basket out the door.

"You don't have to do that, Ama," mumbled the pony man.

"It's all right. I like to be helpful," she called back in.

While he tied the pack baskets to the pony's saddle, he was telling her some story, but she only vaguely listened to him. She really wanted to leave immediately, run away up the trail even, but that would be bad-mannered and would seem suspicious. Instead, she was focusing her attention on several strange, quivering gray welts that covered the pony's pasterns.

"Leeches," said the pony man when he saw her looking at them.

"Leeches? Ugh." They squirmed slightly as they filled on the pony's blood. It was disgusting. So many of them, all bloated with blood. "Can't you take them off?"

"No. Don't try or the pony will kick you." He took his long chopping knife from his gho pocket and touched one of the leeches. The miserable horse kicked its hoof. "They will drink their fill and fall off soon enough. You should check yourself for 'em, too. This place is bad for leeches."

The pony man started off, back south towards Gasa, but she stayed at the muddy meadow for another few moments to settle her nerves and collect her thoughts. It dawned on her that she recognized the knife that the pony man had used to point at the leeches. It was her own one, the one she had left at the little chorten the spring before. The butter, the packets of Wujangs, her knife—they all began making sense to her now.

The fine weather held through November, and life at their camp was easy. Sonam had spun a basket of yak wool while Pema was gone, so she set up her loom and

169

began teacher her daughter to weave the yarn. Gempo returned from Punakha with the winter's supplies, including a shiny new knife for Pema. They played the radio in the evenings until the new batteries went dead. Gempo also brought back a few packs of cigarettes, which he convinced Sonam to smoke with him now and then. Pema was not surprised. Since her trip to Gasa, she was more or less convinced that Kinley and the pony man were behind the chorten and sky burial robberies. Probably Gempo was involved too, wittingly or not. And maybe the soldiers, despite what the dasho said. And she had decided what she was going to do about it: nothing. Preserving her relations with her husbands and the Laya people was more important than any satisfaction that a police investigation would bring. Reporting Kinley or the pony man to the police, whether or not Gempo was implicated, would cut too many of the thin warp threads that connected her to the sparse social fabric of the upper Mo Chhu valley.

Settling her own thoughts and emotions about the shocking events was more difficult, though. It galled her that Kinley—and especially Gempo—could be so deceitful. The thought of Gempo or the pony man collecting the putrefying limbs and fly-blown head and selling them still revolted her. Her desolating sense of loss knowing that "her" chorten was spilled open and empty, and her fear and dread of the evil spawned by the acts still churned inside her. And what about the disgusting leeches at Koina, and, for that matter, the cuckoo's lovely call near Gasa, and Masang Gang, towering above the valley clouds and flashing in the sunshine: what was their connection to the ugly events of the summer? These thoughts chased around and around in her head, not settling themselves down at all, and kept her awake at night. As she went about her daily chores, another thought, that of her mother, also kept coming to mind. Her mother, who in her younger days was as unsophisticated and superstitious as Pema, but who, in

170

her last years spent praying and meditating, had seemed to grow in confidence and serenity. Pema wondered how her mother would have sorted it all out. One day she decided to go back to the ruined chorten and see if any insights from her mother might come to her.

Although the mystery was now more or less explained, it was no easier to approach the chorten than it was during her walk back from Laya. The evil spirits would still be there, swarming like bees from a disturbed hive. Twice she almost resolved to turn back and just forget the whole thing, or come back another day with the dog to protect her. It was the same sort of curiosity to see the sky burial knoll, she remembered, that had started her trouble back during the summer. She hesitated for a moment at the cut-off trail, but then decided it was a duty to her mother, so, mumbling a mantra, forced herself to go on. The chorten was as she had last seen it, its front wall gaping open and its whitewashed stones strewn on the ground. Her first reaction again was to leave, to forget the whole matter, but she took a deep breath and forced herself to sit on the grass for a moment and think. After some time, she found herself glancing past the chorten and across the valley stretched below. It really was a lovely day, after all. The sun was warm on her shoulders. Some bright yellow leaves still hung to the birches along the river, and on the valley slopes the brush had turned russet. Above it all, crystal Masang Gang pierced the blue sky. She listened to the silence, hearing at first only her ears ringing, then the soft swish of a breeze through the fir trees, then a fly buzz past.

She gazed back at the chorten. There it was, nothing more than a little structure of whitewashed stones, some of which happened to be strewn out on the ground. She thought of the girl's remains up on the rocky knoll. There would be snow up there now; the bones would be picked clean, just bones, like the bleached skeletons of blue sheep that she sometimes came across while fetching in yaks. She

171

realized that the images in her mind of tumbled stones and bleached bones, which had until now generated so much fear and aversion and anger, no longer affected her in this way.

She thought again of her mother. A few years before she died, Mother had once reminded Pema that her name, "Pema" meant 'lotus flower,' the beautiful blossom that floated on the surface of muddy ponds, detached from the muck at the bottom. The lotus was permanent and real, her mother had said, the brown water and mud were not. She gazed again up at Masang Gang, where a thin shimmer of snow was now pluming from its peak, frozen in motion. She stood up and stretched and, feeling refreshed, began setting the fallen stones back into the wall of the chorten. Behind one stone her eye caught a little patch of blue color. She knew immediately what it was. The summer's rains had washed off most of its paint, and some of the ashes and clay had dissolved on one side, but unmistakably it was her mother's tsa tsa. She picked it up tenderly and set it back on the ledge under the roof of the chorten.

Glossary

The following non-English language words or phrases are used in the text of the stories to name Bhutanese concepts, expressions, or things for which no adequate corresponding English word exists. The first occurrence of the word in the text of each story is italicized; all subsequent occurrences are printed in regular font. The language in which the word is most commonly associated in Bhutan is listed as: Dz (Dzongkha), Nep (Nepali), Hin (Hindi), or Tib (Tibetan); however, the word may be adopted in other South Asian languages as well.

aamaa (Nep)	mother
ama, am (Dz)	mother, older woman
apa, ap (Dz)	father, older man
ara (Dz)	homemade distilled alcoholic drink of corn, rice or wheat
ashi (Dz)	queen, princess, or general title for high-ranking female
baabaa (Nep)	father
Bagwaan(Nep, Hin)	god

bardo (Dz, Tib)	intermediate period or state between the departure of a dead person's consciousness from his body and its entrances into a new incarnation
bhai (Nep)	younger brother, general address of any young male
bidi (Hin, Nep)	a hand-rolled cigarette or cheap, filterless manufactured cigarette
Chenrezig (Tib)	The Buddha of Compassion (a patron diety of Tibet)
chetrum (Dz)	small denomination coin worth 0.01 ngultrum
chogo (Dz)	yak cheese which is cut into small cubes, hardened, and strung on a cord
chorten (Dz)	a small stone shrine
chutti (Nep)	holiday, day off, weekend
daju (Nep)	older brother, general address for any older male
danyabaad (Nep, Hin)	thank you
dasho (Dz)	the title of high ranking official (literally, "excellent one")
Dasho Dzongda (Dz)	the title of the administrator of a geographical district in Bhutan, analogous to governor
dharma (Dz, Nep)	Buddhist (or Hindu) doctrine
didi (Nep)	older sister, general address for any older woman
doma (Dz)	quid of betel nut with lime paste and betel leaf
dorje / dorji (Dz, Tib)	a ritual object representing the diamond and thunderbolt symbols of Mahayana Buddhism
dramnyen (Dz)	a three-stringed folk instrument, similar to a lute

dratshang (Dz)	the monastic body of a particular area or district
driglam namzha (Dz)	a traditional Bhutanese code of etiquette for dress and respect to superiors, which has been promulgated as national custom
Druk Gylapo (Dz)	the title of the king of Bhutan
duitaa chiyaa (Nep)	"two teas" (e.g. bring two cups of tea)
dzong (Dz)	a fortress / monastery / administrative center, several of which are located at strategic valleys, junctions, etc. throughout Bhutan
gelong (Dz)	an ordained monk
gho (Dz)	a robe worn at knee length; the national costume for men in Bhutan
guru (Hin, Nep)	teacher
Guru Rimpoche (Dz, Tib)	an eighth century AD Buddhist proselytizer who Bhutanese people revere as a patron saint of Bhutan; literally, "precious teacher"
hunchha (Nep)	"it is," "all right," "yes"
Je Khenpo (Dz)	the title of Bhutan's chief abbot
jhidaa (Dz)	a common expletive ("fuck")
julabi (Nep)	a holiday confection made from fried dough and sugar syrup
kabne (Dz)	a ceremonial shawl which men wear as a sign of respect; also a ceremonial scarf which women wear for the same purpose
karom (Dz)	a popular game similar to skittle board

kira (Dz)	an ankle-length wrap dress, the Bhutanese national costume for women
kuru (Dz)	a popular outdoor sport involving throwing large darts at targets
kuzuzampo (Dz)	a traditional greeting, "you are well?"; also, "kuzamo"
la (Dz)	a multipurpose expression denoting respect or politeness
lakh (Nep, Hin)	one hundred thousand
lama (Dz, Tib)	a religious teacher, high-level monk; also, "lam"
Layapa (Dz)	the people of the Laya area of north-central Bhutan
mantra (Dz, Tib)	a prayer
Mahayana	the form of Buddhism practiced in the Himalaya region. Mahayana (or Vajrayana) Buddhism focuses on individual practice of Buddhist virtues in order to eventually, usually over the course of several incarnations, achieve a state of "enlightenment" (i.e. the release from material existence).
namaskar (Nep, Hin)	a respectful greeting, equivalent to "I honor you"
ngultrum (Dz)	The basic unit of Bhutanese currency, at par and interchangeable with the Indian rupee (worth approximately 0.03 U.S. dollars in 1995)
paisa (Nep, Hin)	small denomination coin worth 0.01 rupee

pandit (Hin, Nep)	learned man qualified to perform Hindu rituals
puja (Nep, Dz)	religious ceremony
raamrai chha (Nep)	"good enough"
Sarchopa (Dz)	expression for people from eastern Bhutan, lit. "easterner"
Shabdrung (Dz)	title of the historical head of the Bhutanese religion and state
sinchang (Dz)	a type of homemade millet or barley beer
thangka (Tib, Dz)	a religious image painted, appliquéd, etc. on a fabric scroll
thik chha (Nep)	"that's right," "that's accurate"
thukpa (Dz)	a thick soup of noodles and vegetables or meat
tika (Nep)	a small red dot placed on the forehead to indicate good luck or religious devotion
torma (Tib, Dz)	an elaborately sculpted butter flower used as a religious offering
tsa tsa (Dz)	a small ceramic cone made from mud and the ashes of a deceased person, intended as a memorial to the deceased
tulku (Dz)	a reincarnated lama
wallah (Hin)	a person who does a usual task or job
zee (Dz)	a rare and expensive black and white striped agate
zow (Dz)	a popular snack made from roasted and puffed rice kernels